I0613299

Cold Case Leads To Hot Press

Mark Zeid

ABSOLUTELY AMAZING BOOKS

Manhanset House
Shelter Island Hts., New York 11965-0342

bricktower@aol.com • absolutelyamazingebooks.com

All rights reserved under the International and Pan-American Copyright
Conventions. No part of this publication may be reproduced, stored in a retrieval
system, or transmitted in any form or by any means, electronic, or otherwise, without
the prior written permission of the copyright holder.
The Absolutely Amazing eBooks and Books colophons are trademarks of
J. T. Colby & Company, Inc.

Library of Congress Cataloging-in-Publication Data
Zeid, Mark
Cold Case Leads to Hot Press
p. cm.

1. FICTION / Thrillers / Suspense. 2. FICTION / Mystery & Detective /
Hard-Boiled. 3. FICTION / Thrillers / Crime. Fiction, I. Title.
ISBN: 978-1-955036-88-7, Trade Paper

Copyright © 2025 by Mark Zeid

August 2025

Cold Case Leads To Hot Press

Mark Zeid

ABSOLUTELY AMAZING BOOKS

Habent Sua Fata Libelli

Books by Mark Zeid

Insurance Claims Can Be Murder
Jeff Terrell, Private Investigator, Book One

College Can Be A Killer
Jeff Terrell, Private Investigator, Book Two

Homicide in the Headlines
A Media Murder Mystery, Book One
(A WhoDunIt Award Winner, 2018)

Media Loves Murder and Mayhem
A Media Murder Mystery, Book Two
(A WhoDunIt Award Winner, 2019)

The Age-Old Crime of Murder
(A WhoDunIt Award Winner, 2023)

Dedication

This novel is the result of the efforts of so many individuals and their work to help identify John and Jane Does.

There is Sue Grafton whose novel Q is for Quarry motivated Margaret Press and Colleen Fitzpatrick to create the DNA Doe Project.

Also, Dr. Elizabeth Murray, a forensic pathologist from Southwest Ohio, and her work with law enforcement agencies. She brought forth one of the first successes of the DNA Doe Project with the help of the Miami County Sheriff's Office when they identified the remains of a Jane Doe known as the Buckskin Girl 37 years after she was killed.

However, I wish to dedicate this novel to the Lompoc Jane Doe, the 241st case of the DNA Doe Project, and to the Buckskin Girl, the woman they identified as Marcia King. In addition, let us always keep those other unidentified victims in hearts, minds, and prayers. Hopefully, with the help of science and others, we will learn their names.

Who's Who in
Cold Case Leads to Hot Press

Terry Lambert – copy editor at City Times Newspaper, widowed, he's a dwarf and has a degree in journalism.

Paula Stanford – served six years as a Marine Corps MP, worked as an investigator, pulled a tour in Iraq where wounded and awarded the Silver Star, currently works as a fitness instructor, has issues with her wartime experience.

Becky Watson – young reporter and avid Sherlock Holmes mystery fan.

Marianne Kesler – Jane Doe and first victim, also known as the Sunshine Girl because of the Florida tee shirt she was wearing when found. She was beaten and strangled. Dumped by the road (Marts Hwy) and wrapped in an olive drab green poncho (popular at military surplus stores).

Denise Varney – second victim, also beaten and strangled.

Theresa Hallman – third victim

Tawana Williams – victim who survived her attack but later shot to death.

Cindy Doss – Victim who survived killer's attack.

Detectives David Freedman and Nick Marshall – Marshall is married with a family, Freedman is single, both are seasoned professionals, understanding, intelligent, and appreciate Terry's and Paula's help.

Detective Jennifer Gunn – has a PhD in criminal justice, very intelligent, former Army & served in Iraq.

Detective Steven Oha – third generation Japanese, intelligent, Jennifer's partner.

Donald Belanger – retired game warden, sixty years old, strong, medium build, tall.

Wanda Terrell – science and lifestyle reporter, avid animal lover, crazy about turtles, loves cake – especially carrot cake. Has a dozen turtles and a dog named Tarzan. Husband's name is Larry.

Lynda and John Watson – Becky's parents, John is a doctor (dermatologist).

Bill Fitch – managing editor – old fashion newspaper man, worked as a war correspondent and was nominated twice for a Pulitzer.

Diana Hawley – reporter at City Times, friendly to Terry and helps him with investigations.

Ashford Zane – one of the top reporters for City Times, once nominated for a Pulitzer, a practical joker, not friends with Terry.

Allen Franklin – owner of Stranden's Convenience Store. Bought the place years ago.

Thomas Garcia – veterinarian and someone who dated Becky.

James Whitman – private investigator hired by Tawana Williams.

Vanessa Brown and Beth Jensen – witnesses to an attack.

Randal (Randy) Coffey – boy who witnessed an attack.

[May 1986]

"This is all your fault," the man shouted. He kept his eyes on the road, although every few seconds he would glance over to the slender, young woman wearing a Florida sunshine tee shirt next to him in the cab of the pickup truck. The pretty brunette with long, reddish-brown hair didn't respond.

The road had no streetlights or artificial lighting. It was dark, cave dark, a total and complete absence of light except for the illumination from the car's headlights. The driver saw two red dots ahead. They soon materialized into a lone coyote scurrying across the road.

"I mean look at this from my point of view," the man continued. "I didn't want this to happen. It's all your fault."

The woman's hazelnut-colored eyes continued to stare ahead.

The driver pounded the steering wheel. "You shouldn't have done that."

The driver saw the headlights of another vehicle approaching. He kept moving forward. He didn't want anyone to stop because they thought he was a stranded motorist. The car passed him, going in the opposite direction. The driver watched until the car's rear lights were out of sight.

The driver brought his pickup to a stop. *Yes, this is a good spot,* he thought. *There are no lights. There's very little traffic, so I can stop on the pavement and not have to pull over onto the shoulder of road and stay out of the dirt. I have to be careful not to leave footprints, but that's not difficult. The good thing is there's a ditch to help hide her. Yes, this is the perfect spot to dump the body.*

∞∞∞∞∞∞

CHAPTER ONE
[thirty-four years later, day one]

A tall woman wearing a stylish sweat suit stepped off the elevator into the editorial office of *City Times Newspaper*. People were seated at their desks talking to those next to them instead of working on computers. Several were watching one of the four large TV monitors on the wall. The tall woman with shoulder-length blond hair took a few steps in one direction, searching for her quarry. Not finding him in that section of the room, she advanced to another part of the office. Still, the person of her quest was not in sight. She kept shifting her weight from one foot to another, searching. She was becoming frustrated by her lack of success.

"Hey Paula," a voice behind her said. "What took you so long?"

Paula Stafford turned to face a man standing a bit less than four feet tall. "Give me a break Terry. What is so important that I had to come here? What couldn't you tell me over the phone?"

Terry Lambert took a deep breath and pulled Paula aside, out of earshot of the others in the room. "Something terrible has happened."

"What?"

"It's Becky."

"Becky? Little Miss Sunshine who loves everybody? What could possibly be the problem with her?"

Terry sighed. "The worst kind. She's been shot."

∞∞∞∞∞∞

Hospitals all have the same smell. It's one of antiseptic and cleaning solutions trying to hide odors from vomit, blood, and other bodily functions. There are the sounds of machines beeping; beds being wheeled around; medical personnel calling over the intercom for medicine, medical procedures, or equipment; and people crying when doctors or nurses tell them the results of procedures. There are children crying and whining because of their discomfort and boredom along with mothers complaining about the length of time it takes for a doctor to see them and their child. The hallways function as natural megaphones to amplify every smell and sound.

Paula took a deep breath and let it out slowly as she and Terry entered the ER waiting room. Surprise and shock didn't often come to Paula Stanford. Her combat experience in Iraq as a military police officer for the Marine Corps prepared her for news of friends being wounded or killed. But this time it was different. Becky wasn't a combat casualty. "Who would do such a thing? Becky is one of the sweetest people I know. Why would anyone want to shoot her?"

"Don't know," Terry replied. "All the police told us was she was leaving her apartment when someone shot her. We really don't know anything about what happened or how she is."

"Someone shot her at her apartment. What did she do that would make a person want to kill her?"

"Kill her?" Terry asked with disbelief.

"This person targeted her. She was not shot by accident. Whoever shot her wanted her dead. We're lucky that she's still alive, and we can only hope and pray for her."

"Is that it?"

"What do you expect?"

Terry took a deep breath. "I was kind of hoping you would be able to help us do a bit more."

Paula furrowed her eyebrows. "Do a bit more? Like what? I mean I like Becky, but we really aren't that close. She works with you at the newspaper. You're a lot closer to her than I am."

"Yes, I know. But she's been shot. You're the only person I can think of who's dealt with people being wounded. I don't know what to do or how to help her."

"Be there for the family," Paula replied. "Honestly, it's the doctor and nurses who are going to help her. You need to focus on helping the family deal with this."

"What about you?" Terry asked. "Will you help us? You know Becky. You like her. She helped us with that serial killer last year. I really need your help with this."

Paula groaned. "Okay. I'll help. Why not? You're right. I actually do like the kid."

Terry looked around the waiting room before touching Paula's arm and motioning to a middle-aged couple. "Come on. Let me introduce you to Becky's parents." They approached the couple. "Paula, this here is Doctor John Watson and his wife, Lynda. They're Becky's parents." Terry faced the Watsons. " This is Paula Stanford. She's a good friend of Becky's."

Paula stepped forward and extended her hand to Dr. Watson. "Becky often talked about you. She told me you're a Sherlock Holmes fan. You turned her into one too."

"Well," Dr. Watson replied with a grin. "Being named John Watson, it was only natural I became a fan. And you can believe I get plenty of ribbing from my patients about my name."

Paula gave him a slight nod. "I wish our meeting was under better circumstances."

"So do I," Dr. Watson answered.

"I can't believe it," Paula said, letting out a long sigh. "Who would want to shoot Becky?" Paula watched as Becky's parents nodded and walked away to find space alone where they could comfort each other. She searched for a seat before she sat down. Terry took a seat next to her.

"I think they design these things to be as uncomfortable as possible," Terry said as he squirmed in the chair. "Probably so people will get up and pace around."

"I'm sure they do," Paula replied. "If you're that uncomfortable, let's go and get some coffee," Paula suggested.

Paula stood up and motioned for Terry to join her. She followed the signs to the hospital cafeteria. Terry stopped at the entrance.

"What's the matter?" Paula asked. "I know it's not the chairs."

"Bad memories," Terry answered. He motioned with his hand that they should go ahead. They went through the line picking up pastry and coffee. They found an empty table.

Paula sat down and leaned back in her chair. "Bad memories? You and me both. Want to talk about it?"

Terry stared at Paula. "Talk about what?"

"Your bad memories."

Terry took a sip of coffee and took a deep breath. "Not really."

"I tell the VA counselor the same thing. But she insists I tell her anyway. It's supposed to help."

Terry took a deep breath. "I doubt it. It's personal."

"Of course it is. You wouldn't be upset if it wasn't. Come on. Tell me. I promise it will remain between the two of us."

Terry took a moment to consider Paula's advice. "Five years ago, my wife," Terry began slowly. "Kristen was killed in a traffic accident. The driver of the car that t-boned her was drunk and here in this hospital because of his injuries. I tried to go up to his room, to confront him. The police stopped me. I spent two weeks here in the hospital trying to see him. I spent a lot of time in this very cafeteria. Every time I tried to see him; the staff stopped me. I tried to see him when he was released, but the police kept him in pretrial custody, and I wasn't allowed to have any contact with him. He made a plea deal and served three years. He took my wife from me and he spent three years for being drunk and killing her."

"Is that why you don't drive? I noticed you don't have a car."

Before Terry could answer, Detectives Nick Marshall and David Freedman entered the cafeteria and walked over to him and Paula.

Marshall was lean and a natural athlete. He won a baseball scholarship, which got him through college. After college, he tried out for a professional team but wasn't quite good enough. He was still an avid fan of the game. Many said the only time he was in a good mood was when he was watching a baseball game, a pastime he enjoyed sharing with his two children. Freedman was tall, muscular, extremely easy-going, and at least ten years younger than Marshall. His good looks and being a bachelor made him extremely popular among the single women at the police department.

"Good to see you," Marshall said as he and Freedman approached Paula and Terry. "I take it you're down here because of your friend being shot."

"What a marvelous deduction," Paula responded sarcastically. "You should be a detective. Oh, wait, you are. Now, tell us what happened. Who did this? Why did they do it?"

"Actually, I'm hoping you could tell me," Marshall said, waving his hand toward Terry. "Here's what we know. Your friend was coming out of her apartment, probably going to work. Witnesses said someone in a dark SUV called out to her. She approached the vehicle and the driver shot her twice, then sped off. A couple of people were on the street, but they didn't get a look at the driver and didn't really notice the SUV until they heard the shots. They rushed over to help your friend. One of them called for an ambulance. Your friend was lucky. Between first aid one of the bystanders gave her and the quick response from the EMTs, they were able to keep her alive until she got here. We're also fortunate that Fort Stebbins is a large enough city to have a first-rate trauma center. What's her status?"

"We don't know," Paula replied. "We're waiting. I know Becky's parents have been here for several hours. I guess it's a good sign. It means she's still in surgery. Why don't we talk to her parents? They may have some news on Becky." She and Terry stood up and started for the exit.

"Good idea," Marshall said as he and Freedman followed Paula and Terry out of the cafeteria back to the waiting room.

"I'm assuming you've processed the crime scene and canvassed the neighborhood. Did you find anything?" Paula asked as they walked to the ER waiting room.

Marshall groaned. "Yes, and no. We didn't find anything. And trust me when I tell you we went over the scene with a fine-tooth comb. Nothing. Nada. Not a thing. As for canvassing the neighborhood, that was easy. It seemed everyone who knew your friend was more than eager to talk to us. Again, nothing. We even looked for cameras in the neighborhood. There were a few and we're reviewing the footage; but so far, nothing. All we know is someone drove up to your friend's place and shot her. The only real lead we have is she was targeted, someone wanted to kill her. Now, would you know of any reason for someone to hurt your friend?"

"First of all, her name is Becky," Paula curtly answered. "And no, I don't know why anyone would want to hurt her. To tell you the truth, Becky is one of the sweetest people I know. I can't imagine anyone wanting to hurt her."

"That's what her neighbors said," Freedman added. "They said she was the kind of person who went out of her way to be nice to everyone."

"Let's look at this differently," Marshall said being sure to address Terry. "Maybe it was something she was working on. Can you think of anything she was working on that would have caused someone to want to hurt her?"

Terry shook his head. "Not that I can think of. She's fairly new; she's been with us for less than a year, so she wouldn't be doing any kind of investigative reporting. Have you talked to her parents? They might know something. I can introduce you to them. They're here in the ER waiting room."

"Please. Still, we'll want to check her files," Marshall stated. "Can you help us with that?"

Before Terry could answer, a middle-aged doctor in scrubs came into the waiting room. He immediately approached John and Lynda Watson.

Paula rushed over to the doctor. "Are you the doctor who operated on Becky Watson? How is she?"

The doctor took a step back. "Excuse me, but who are you?"

"I'm Paula Stanford, Becky's friend. Please tell me how's she doing."

The doctor put up his hands. "I'm sorry, but I can't give out information about a patient without her consent. The only people I can talk to are her family. In this case, it's Dr. Watson and his wife."

Marshall stepped up and put himself between the doctor and Paula, forcing her to back up. "I'm Detective Nick Marshall with the Fort Stebbins Police Department. We're all concerned about Ms. Watson. I'll need to talk to you about getting information for our investigation."

"Of course," the doctor replied. "But first, I must talk to Dr. Watson and his wife."

Marshall and Freedman pulled Paula and Terry aside while the surgeon informed Becky's parents of her condition. As soon as the surgeon stepped away, Paula along with Terry, Marshall and Freedman approached Becky's parents.

"What did the doctor say?" Paula demanded.

John was holding Lynda, who was trying to hold back her tears. "He told us Becky was brought in with two gunshot wounds to her chest. They were able to remove the bullets, which they will turn over to the police. They were also able to stop the bleeding. But she went into cardiac arrest while on the operating table. Of course, they were able to restart her heart. But Becky is in critical condition. Still, she's young and strong, so there's hope she will recover."

"Can we see her?" Paula pleaded

"She in the ICU. She's still unconscious. They're keeping her in a medically induced coma. It will help her rest and heal. Right now, there isn't anything you can do. Lynda and I are going in to see her. If you make sure I have your contact information, I'll call you if there is any change."

"Is anything we can do for you and Becky?" Terry asked.

"Not at this time, but thank you for your consideration," John answered.

Paula took a deep breath and nodded that she understood. She led Terry away from Becky's parents. "Now's not the time to visit her. It's better if we let her parents spend some time alone with her. In the meantime, let's find the son of a bitch who shot Becky."

∞∞∞∞∞∞

One good thing about hospital waiting rooms is wher. they are crowded, no one really notices you. Yes, you're on security cameras; but if you don't do anything to attract attention, it's like you're a part of the furniture. That's the way he liked it. It seemed natural to the other occupants in the room for an old man to be alone, waiting for news about a loved one or the results of some medical tests.

There was a tall blond woman in a track suit. With her was a really short guy. They made an odd couple. Probably friends. There was an older couple who seemed to know the other two. It didn't take long before he realized they were there for the same reason he was. He wanted to know how the young blond who was shot this morning was doing.

After several hours, a couple of detectives arrived. That caused him some concern. Then, a doctor came out and told the older couple the patient's condition. Like the parents, he wasn't pleased about what he had heard. The patient was still alive.

CHAPTER TWO

The news stops for no one. Another reporter filled in for Terry, editing the stories reporters submitted. Other reporters were on their phones or their computers either researching facts or writing articles. Several reporters were chatting next to the coffee maker. All this came to a halt when Terry walked in. Terry stood quietly by the elevator.

Bill Fitch, the managing editor came out of his office. Even at sixty plus years and an expanding waistline, he was still an imposing figure. Of course, being more than six feet tall helped. "Well, don't just stand there," he bellowed. This guy was never going to get lost in a fog. It seemed the only volume Fitch spoke in was loud, very loud. "How is she? What happened? Have they caught the guy who shot her?"

Terry took a deep breath. "First of all, Becky had surgery and they removed two bullets. The doctors say she has a chance, but her condition is critical. As for what happened, no one really knows. She was coming out of her apartment when someone in an SUV shot her. Why? No one knows. The police are investigating, but they have no leads yet. The only thing I can ask is for everyone to keep Becky in your prayers."

Terry walked to his desk and sat down. He was conscious of others in the office watching him before they slowly resumed their work for the paper. Fitch went over to Terry and handed him a piece of paper. "I want you to write up what happened to Becky for tomorrow's paper."

"What?" yelled Terry. "We're making Becky tomorrow's headline. What kind of person are you?"

"I'm the managing editor and I'm telling you to write up what happened. You know more than anyone else about what's going on. And before you get so bent out of shape, why don't you read that paper I just gave you?"

Terry unfolded the paper. After reading it he looked up at Fitch.

"That's right," Fitch said. "The paper is offering a ten-thousand-dollar reward for any news that leads to the arrest and conviction of the person who shot Becky. This time it's not about headlines but catching the shooter." Fitch quieted down and put his hand on Terry's shoulder. "I really need you to write this up. You have that special ability to make the story about the person and not sensationalism."

"What about other news agencies?" Diana asked from her desk. "I'm sure TV news stations have called and are making this their lead story for tonight. Isn't Terry's story going to piss them off? It looks like we're hoarding information and focusing on getting an exclusive instead of sharing information and answering their queries."

"We've been able to hold them off for now," Fitch answered. "We've said we need to notify the family first before issuing any statement. We also referred them to the police department's public information officer. As for Terry's story, it's about what we are doing to support the police and find the shooter. The only thing we're publishing beyond what the police are saying is that we are offering a reward. We've notified the police and they will issue a statement about it. To be honest, until Terry walked in, the police knew more about what was happening than we did."

The elevator opened and out stepped Marshall and Freedman. The entire newsroom turned its attention to the new intruders.

"Greetings and salutations," Freedman playfully said as he spread out his arms. "What a pleasure to see you all."

Fitch approached the detectives. "Make like the Jolly Green Giant and can the crap. What do you want? Why are you here?"

Marshall looked at Freedman. "I can really feel the warmth, can't you?" he said. He turned his attention back to Fitch. "Your reporter was shot in front of her apartment this morning. The hospital turned over the bullets they removed from her. Whoever did it, targeted her. Someone wanted her dead. Now, we're lucky in that she is still alive and hopefully she'll be able to tell us who tried to kill her when she regains consciousness. Until then, why not let us check her files? Maybe we can find out who shot her."

"Not without a warrant," Fitch demanded. "Make no mistake. We will cooperate fully with your investigation. But it has got to be by the book. When you catch whoever did this, I don't want him to get off on some damn technicality. Get me a warrant, and I will give you her files."

Marshall pulled a folded piece of paper from his pocket. "I figured as much. Here's your warrant. Now give us the files."

Fitch took the paper from Marshall and examined it. "Everything seems in order."

"Great, give us the files," Marshall ordered.

"It's not that simple," Terry interjected. "Becky's files are on her computer. We need her password to access it."

"I can take care of that," a portly woman replied.

"You are?" Marshall asked.

"Detectives, I want you to meet Ms. Wanda Terrell," Fitch said with a wave of his hand.

Wanda was rather unique. She had a degree in chemistry and knew just about everyone at the university and in certain circles. However, what most people found fascinating about her was her love of carrot cake and turtles. She had about a dozen turtles at her home, which she shared with her husband and a large mixed-breed dog, or as she liked to call it, a pure-breed mutt with lots of love. Everyone was also sure there was at least one carrot cake in her home.

"What can I do to help you detectives?" Wanda asked. "I heard about what happened this morning. It's terrible, just terrible."

"We're hoping to access Ms. Watson's files to see if she was working anything that would have gotten her shot," Marshall said as he approached Wanda.

"Well, I can access her files. If you give me about an hour, I'll make you a copy of them."

Marshall exhaled loudly. "I'd rather you just supplied us with her password. We'll take the computer with us and download everything. I can assure you that we won't delete anything or reveal any trade secrets."

Wanda motioned for Marshall to have a seat in the chair at Becky's desk. "Have at it, and good luck. If you need any assistance, just come and get me. Her password is 2-2-1-capital-B-capital-B-a-k-e-r capital S-t-r-e-e-t, 221B Baker Street."

"Interesting," Marshall commented. "How come you know her password?"

"It's a secret," Wanda answered coyly.

"Her and Becky are really good friends," Terry whispered to Marshall and Freedman.

Marshall watched Wanda as she returned to her desk. "I wonder what other secrets she knows about Ms. Watson."

∞∞∞∞∞

"Find anything?" Terry asked after Marshall and Freedman spent two hours going through all her computer files and every piece of paper they found on top of Becky's desk and in the drawers.

"Yeah," Marshall answered. "She likes cats and Chinese food. Other than that, nothing. Although, there were several notes with a phone number about someone called Tom. Know who he is?"

Terry shrugged his shoulders. "No idea. It could have been someone she interviewed for a story she worked on."

"How about the stories she worked on? We didn't find anything of interest in her files."

"I searched all the stories she submitted since she started working here," Terry answered. "She did mostly puff pieces, stories about an animal shelter, a commune with a community garden, a charity and how it's helping the community, that kind of stuff. Everything she wrote was about how great they were. Nothing that would make anyone angry, certainly not cause anyone to want to kill her. You know, she used to work as a waitress at Murphy's before here. Maybe it's someone from there that wants to kill her."

"How long has she been working here?" Freedman asked.

"For about eight months."

Freedman made a note of Terry's answer. "We'll be sure to check that out. What about boyfriends?" he asked. "Jilted lovers? Stalkers? Anyone hanging around the paper trying to meet her, etc.?"

"Give me a minute," Terry replied. He left the detectives but returned a few minutes later with Wanda. Wanda smiled and greeted the detectives.

"You're friends with Becky," Terry stated. "Can you tell us about any of her boyfriends?"

"Oh, Dearie. I don't like to gossip."

"Wanda," Terry said with a bit of frustration. "You're the society reporter. Your job is basically gossiping about famous people."

The portly woman crossed her arms. "Now don't you give me attitude. And I'm the science and lifestyle reporter, not a gossip columnist."

Terry mumbled an apology.

"Excuse me," Marshall interjected. "Because of the attack on Ms. Watson, we're trying to find out if she had any enemies, jealous boyfriend, jilted lover, etc. Can you help us with that?"

Wanda dropped her arms and turned to face Marshall. "Well, Becky and I are friends. I do know she was dating this one young man. I don't know how serious they were, but I don't think he would hurt her."

Marshall picked up a pad of paper. "You got a name?"

"Well," Wanda answered coyly smiling, "he's a very handsome Hispanic gentleman named Thomas Garcia. He's a veterinarian. His office is on Fourth Avenue, next to The Red Vine Wine Shop. You can't miss it."

"Thanks," Marshall replied as he looked at his watch, then Freedman. "It's getting late. Don't think we'll catch him at his office today."

Freedman disconnected the cables to the computer and picked it up. He handed Terry a form. "Here's a receipt for Ms. Watson's computer and the materials we're taking with us. Once we've gone through all the files again, we'll return everything."

"Not a problem," Terry answered. Holding the receipt for Becky's computer and files, Terry watched the two detectives get on the elevator and leave. A strange feeling came over him. Somehow, he knew the answer to who shot Becky was not in that computer.

CHAPTER THREE
[day two]

"Please, someone open the windows," Detective Marshall cried out before he entered the two-bedroom apartment. "What do we have here?" he asked the patrol officer who kept a record of people who entered and left the crime scene.

"Homicide," answered the patrol officer, "victim's been dead for about a week."

"Well, that explains the odor," Detective Freedman said waving his hand in front of his face to dispel the odor.

"What," Marshall said sarcastically. "You don't like starting the day with a week-old, dead body? What's gotten into you?"

"I'm used to fresh country air," Freedman replied. "You know the kind where you can smell bull. . ."

"For miles. Yeah, I know," Marshall said.

A patrol officer put a small fan in a window he opened to help get rid of the odor of decomposition.

The detectives put on white protective coveralls, commonly called *bunny suits,* to protect their clothes from the odor and getting any stains on them. Marshall took one of the surgical face masks from the box next to the entrance. He took a little bit of Vicks VapoRub from the jar next to the masks and rubbed it under his nose. Freedman did the same and followed Marshall into the apartment to find the coroner, also wearing a bunny suit and a surgical mask, kneeling next to a blackened, bloated corpse. "Well Doc, what's the verdict?"

"Looks like she bled out from two gunshot wounds to her chest. Can't tell for sure, but I wouldn't be surprised if time of death was a week ago."

"Got an ID?" Freedman asked.

The coroner pointed to a purse on a side table. Next to it were an ash tray full of cigarette butts, a cell phone, a wallet, and a driver's license. "According to her license, her name is Tawana Williams, age forty-eight. One of the patrol officers is running a check to see if she has a record."

As on cue, a patrol officer entered the apartment, covering his face with his arm to shield himself from the odor. He handed Freedman a sheet of paper before coughing as he left. "She has a record," Freedman said. "She was picked up for prostitution several times in the late 1990s. A couple of assault complaints, but nothing for the past twenty-five years. Turns out she had an alias, 'Sweet Tea' when she was working the streets."

Marshall looked around the apartment. Except for the dead body in the middle of the living room floor, the place was clean and uncluttered. "Wonder what she's doing now if she isn't turning tricks? Nothing fancy about the place, but I'm sure she pays the rent somehow."

Freedman put on a pair of nitrile gloves and examined the contents of the victim's purse. He pulled out a pay stub. "This says she's employed at the Pink Lily Lounge. Probably either a waitress or a bartender."

"You sure about that?" Marshall questioned. "She could be a stripper."

"It's not that kind of place," Freedman answered. "I've been there. It's more of a blues and jazz club. They have live music on the weekends."

"Didn't know you were a jazz fan," said Marshall.

"There's a lot you don't know about me."

"Lucky me." Marshall said. "Do me a favor and keep it a secret." He turned to one of the patrol officers. "Who found her?"

"The mailman. He was dropping off a package, he noticed the odor and recognized it as decomp. Turns out this isn't the first time he's found a dead body."

"Where's the package?" Freedman asked.

The patrol officer pointed to a box setting on the kitchen table.

Freedman went over and examined the box. According to the label, it was a package containing cosmetics. He made a mental note to take the package into evidence and check the contents. "What about notifying next of kin? Has anyone done that?"

"Not yet," the patrol officer answered. "It seems she lived here alone."

"We'll take care of it," Marshall replied. "We have to talk to them anyway."

The coroner stood up and motioned for his two assistants to come and take the body away.

Marshall tapped the coroner on the shoulder. "Make sure to get the bullets to ballistics. After that, we'll put the information into ViCAP (Violent Criminal Apprehension Program) and NIBIN (National Integrated Ballistic Information Network)."

The coroner gave him a thumbs-up sign before leaving with the body.

CHAPTER FOUR

The gym opened at five in the morning and closed at ten in the evening, something Paula appreciated. She was able to work out before or after the exercise classes she taught here. Not that it really mattered; she had a key to the place. She couldn't sleep, so at five that morning she decided it was time for her to go to the gym and work off some of her anger. She grabbed her German shepherd, Keiko, before leaving the apartment. While Paula spent time hitting and kicking a heavy bag, Keiko found a corner to lie down. Another perk of working here, Sam, the owner, allowed her to bring her dog into the gym. Keiko was quite popular with the members. Paula was still pounding on the bag when she heard someone behind her.

"What did that bag ever do to you?" the voice asked.

Keiko got up to greet the intruder. Paula turned to see Terry in the doorway. He was dressed in a blue tracksuit that had seen better days. "Where did you get that outfit?"

Terry spread out his arms and turned around to model it for her. "Like it? I've had it since college." Keiko made it a point to sniff it in several places. She backed up two steps and barked.

"Ever think of buying a new one? Even Keiko thinks you should get a new one."

Terry dropped his arms. "What does your dog know? Do you know how hard it is to find anything in my size? Trust me, once you get something, you wear it until it's falling apart."

Paula scoffed. "It's falling apart."

Terry looked at his attire. "I guess I should invest in a new one. But it's so hard to find a place selling clothes that fit me."

Paula grinned. "I hadn't thought about that. I mean I'm tall, so I should know how hard it is to find clothes that fit. So, why are you here?"

"Why are you here?" Terry asked as he entered the room and set down his gym bag. Keiko followed him and started sniffing the gym bag.

"Couldn't sleep, so I thought I would come in early and get a workout in. Why are you here at. . .? What time is it?"

"According to the clock in the lobby, it's six twenty."

"Awfully early for you to come here to exercise."

"I'm here for the same reason you are," Terry said.

"You're pissed, and you want to beat the crap out of something," Paula said as she grabbed a bottle of water.

"Bingo," Terry replied. "Also, I figured it wouldn't hurt for me to review some of those self-defense moves you taught me a while back."

"Hey, how did you know I would be here?"

"I didn't. I was just hoping you would be. I knew the gym was open, so I figured it wouldn't hurt. If you weren't here, I could exercise. If you were, then you could show me some more self-defense moves."

"You're not scared that someone is coming after you, are you?"

"Hey, I'm not like you: a decorated combat veteran and a former Marine Corps military police officer," Terry snidely answered. "Who knows why someone wanted to hurt Becky? It's quite possible all of us are in danger."

"I doubt he is after you, or anyone else," Paula said to reassure him.

"Why do you say that?"

Paula shrugged her shoulders. "Don't know. Guess it just doesn't make any sense. If someone was targeting the newspaper, I doubt they would start with shooting a junior reporter."

"Then let me do what you're doing."

"What's that?"

Terry clenched his fist and hit the heavy bag. "Like I said, I'm here for the same reason you are. I want to hit something. I'm angry and I want to beat the crap out of something."

Paula chuckled. "Then come on, Tiger. Let's do it to it. I have an early morning class in an hour, so until then, let's see what you can do."

∞∞∞∞∞∞

"Yea! We survived another workout," one of the women in the exercise class said while catching her breath. "Now I can enjoy having donuts with my morning coffee without guilt."

"Well, I was kind of hoping you enjoyed the class," Paula replied. "The goal is to find some type of exercise you enjoy so that you will continue to do it. Not to exercise so that you can cheat on your diet. Look at joggers. Most of them enjoy running and getting outside. That's why they continue to do it all their lives."

"Oh, we do enjoy the class," another one of the ladies said. "It's just that it's a lot harder for us than it is for you. But you didn't seem to enjoy it."

"It's not that," Paula answered. "I'm dealing with a personal issue at the moment."

"Oh, my goodness," one of the ladies said. "What is it dear? Maybe we can help."

"I doubt it. I have a friend in the hospital, and I'm really worried about her."

"Oh, my goodness, what happened?"

"No, it's okay. I hate to bother you with my problems."

"Nonsense, we care about you. We're your friends as well as people who come to work out with you. Now, tell us what happened."

"My friend was shot yesterday as she left her apartment. No one knows why, but the police are investigating."

The women grabbed Paula's hand and let her know they wanted to support her. "If you tell us her name, we'll pray for her," one of the women said.

"That's sweet of you." Paula had little faith in prayer, but she gave the women a smile for the support her students had for her. "Her name is Becky Watson. I'm sure she'll appreciate your kindness."

One of the women gave Paula a hug. "We're happy to do it. God loves those who care about others. Now you take care, dear." Several of the women also gave Paula a hug before they left.

Paula waved at them as they left the room.

Keiko followed Paula as she put away the equipment she used during the class. When she finished, she noticed Sam Adkins, the owner of the gym, standing in the doorway.

"Hey Sam. What's up? Also, sorry about yesterday, but I had to take care of a personal issue." Keiko, wanting attention, went over to Sam.

Sam was a retired semi-pro football player who still managed to work out with weights several times a week. But age was catching up with him and while he still had the muscles, he was developing a slight paunch which he tried to hide by wearing very loose untucked tee shirts. "Need to talk to you, Paula," he said as he ruffled the fur around Keiko's neck.

"Sure, what's the problem?"

"With you, none. With the others here, again, nothing. Everyone here is great."

"Even me being late and out yesterday?"

"Hey, I understand. You had a friend in the hospital, and you had to be there for her. Not a problem."

"But," Paula said slowly. "It's not Keiko, is it?" Keiko's ears perked up at the mention of her name.

"No, No. everyone loves her." Sam sighed and took a deep breath. "It's my mother. She lives in Anaheim, California."

"Know the place. I was stationed at Camp Pendleton."

"Well, my dad died about two years ago. Since then, she's been having a tough time of it, also with her health problems, well, things haven't been going well for her."

"Sorry to hear that. But what do you need from me?"

Sam took another deep breath before answering. "My wife and I are going to move out there and take care of her. Our kids are grown. There's just the two of us; so, it will be easy for us to relocate."

"California's expensive. Why not bring her here and set her up in an assisted living facility?"

"Thought about it, but it turns out, I miss California. Besides, it will be easier on her to stay where she is."

"And what happens to the gym?"

"That's the issue. I'm selling it. I've got enough to retire, and it's about time I did. So, I'm putting the gym up for sale."

"Who's buying it? Is it one of those fitness franchises?"

Sam shrugged his shoulders. "No one yet, I just put it on the market. But after today, I'm closing the place down for a couple of weeks to take inventory and have an inspection of the place. I also need to get the books in order. After that, I should have an idea of what it's worth."

Paula crossed her arms and took a minute to collect her thoughts. "What about us, the people who work here?"

Sam nodded. "Well, Kathy will be helping me with the inventory and getting things in order. After that, I'll reopen the gym until I get an offer, so you're all still employed. But I wanted to give everyone fair warning as to what to expect. I care about all of you. I hate to leave, but I have my mother to think of. I just can't keep this place. You understand, don't you?"

Paula forced a smile and put her hand on Sam's arm. "Of course, I understand. Family should always come first. I appreciate you letting me know what's going to happen. I'm just hoping I still have a job when the new owner takes over."

"Oh, I'm sure you will. You're our best instructor. Everyone likes you."

"Thanks, Sam." Paula gave him another smile before grabbing Keiko's leash and putting it on her. "I appreciate the heads up. Keep me informed of what happens when you sell the place."

"Hey," Sam loudly stated. "Until then you still have a job. Don't forget that. I will take care of you and all my employees."

Sam waved as Paula left the gym.

CHAPTER FIVE

Terry entered the editorial office. The hour he spent with Paula, punching the bag and exercising, felt good, relieving a lot of the frustration from being unable to do anything for Becky. He knew he would have lots of sore muscles the next day. Still, the workout placed him in a good mood. Terry placed his gym bag with his workout clothes under his desk. He sat down and picked up a photo of an attractive brunette. He gently touched the photograph of his wife, Kristen, as he continued to stare at it, remembering the years they had spent together before that tragic accident that took her life.

Terry jumped when a hand touched his shoulder. He turned around to face Wanda.

Wanda was startled and jumped back. "Sorry, I didn't mean to scare you."

"Well, you did," Terry said loudly as he placed the photograph back on his desk. "You scared the holy crap out of me."

"You know, that is a very interesting point."

"What is?"

"Holy crap," Wanda replied. "Think about it. Is there really such a thing as holy crap? I mean, when a priest or the Pope takes a crap, is it holy?"

Terry gave her a confused look. "Wanda, don't take this the wrong way, but you have a weird way of thinking. Now, was there a reason you came over here, other than to scare me?"

"Well, someone had sour milk with his coffee this morning."

"Sorry Wanda. It's just with Becky in the hospital, I'm touchy about everything."

"That's why I came over here. I'm going to visit her as soon as I leave here."

"Good. Let us know how she's doing."

Wanda handed Terry a flash drive. "Will do. Also, I copied her files from her computer."

"How did you get her files?"

"I downloaded them before the cops showed up. Wanted to have a backup in case the police took her computer. Figured they would, so I made an extra copy of her files for you. I figured you and your friend, Paula, could use it to find out what is going on and who shot Becky."

Terry started to put the flash drive into his computer. Wanda reached over and stopped him. "Don't," she said. "It's best that no one here knows you have it. If it was one of Becky stories that got her shot, then you really don't want anyone to know you have her files."

"Why not?" Terry asked. "People know the police took Becky's computer."

Wanda picked up her bag and walked to the elevator. She pressed the button and turned to face Terry. "The police can take care of themselves. What I don't want is for the killer to know anyone here at the paper has that information. We don't need another reporter getting shot." The elevator arrived, Wanda stepped on and waved goodbye.

∞∞∞∞∞

Paula stared at the diploma on the wall, Cathy Jeffers, Doctor of Psychology. Paula couldn't make up her mind whether she liked or hated the woman. The therapist listened and understood, gave good advice, and was usually right on the money with it. That's what Paula hated. Paula didn't like coming to the VA Mental Health Clinic; but it kept her from going nuts. Exercise and medication could only do so much for Paula's PTSD. The forty-year-something therapist with short brown hair walked in and took her seat behind the desk. Paula sat down in a chair in front of Cathy's desk. Paula was impressed with the woman's youthful look, including freckles which enhanced her pale skin and good looks.

"So, what's new with you?" the therapist asked.

"Well Dr. Jeffers. . ."

"No, no," the woman interrupted. "It's Cathy. Call me Cathy."

Another thing Paula didn't like. "Well Cathy, it's been a very stressful week."

"Why is that?"

Paula took a deep breath. "First, a friend of mine was shot. She's now in the hospital."

"Oh, how terrible. How is she?"

Paula wished the woman would quit interrupting. "She's in critical condition. To be quite honest, there's a chance she may die." Paula stopped talking.

"I'm sorry to hear about your friend. Can you tell me more? What happened? Were you there? Did the police catch the guy who shot her?"

Paula put up her hand to quiet Cathy. "I wasn't there. My friend was coming out of her apartment building when someone shot her. The police don't know who or why."

"How are you doing? I know you're upset. What are you doing to deal with this situation?"

"Punching the crap out of a punching bag."

"Well, that's a healthy way of dealing with frustration. What else?"

"I'm also dealing with possibly losing my job."

Cathy waited for Paula to explain. "Can you tell me why you are losing your job?"

"The owner is selling the place," Paula answered. "He's moving to California to take care of his mother, who has health problems. Anyway, he's selling the place. No one knows what will happen once it's sold. But there is a good chance everyone working there will be out of a job."

Cathy leaned back in her chair and put her hands together in front of her face. "How are you handling this? Are you punching a bag in the gym to deal with this?"

"Yeah. It helps when I'm at work. But afterwards, I tend to stress out."

"And how do you deal with the stress?"

"Try to relax, mellow out."

"Are you drinking to mellow out?"

"Of course, I'm drinking," Paula yelled. "What do you expect me to do?"

"I'm sorry, I didn't mean to upset you. Let's see if we can't find ways to help you deal with the issues you are facing. Having different options may help you deal with your problems. The goal is for us to find ways to help you."

"I drink so that I can sleep. It's either alcohol or pills. So, tell me, which one is better?"

"So, you are still having problems with insomnia?"

"I didn't say that."

"Yes, you did." The therapist and Paula sat quietly, staring at each other. After a moment, Cathy broke the silence. "You're angry and upset. It's natural. What we need to do is figure out is a healthy way of dealing with these issues, a plan of action."

"A plan of action," Paula shouted. "Just what do you want me to do? My friend is in the hospital and I'm going to be out of work. These things are out of my control."

"Yes, those things are out of your control. So, we need to come up with a plan of action focusing on what you can do."

Paula stood up and grabbed her bag. "Okay, here's my plan of action. I'm going to get drunk. Then I'm going to find the son of a bitch who shot my friend." Before Cathy could respond, Paula stormed out of the office.

∞∞∞∞∞∞

He couldn't believe how easy it was for him to get into the ICU. He picked up a small bouquet of flowers to make everyone think he was visiting a patient. He was, but not to encourage any kind of recovery. He found the young reporter's room, with all kinds of wires and tubes connecting her to several machines.

He looked around the room to see if there was a way to kill her without attracting the attention of the nurses' station. He knew people at the nurses' station monitored the machines continuously. He needed to create a distraction to get the nurses away from the monitors for a few minutes. The easiest way was to turn off the machines for another patient, forcing the staff to rush to that person's aid. He moved down the hall, carefully looking into each room as he passed it. After several minutes, he found an unconscious patient alone. He quietly went in and waited a moment before pulling the leads off the person's chest. He exited the room quickly and managed to find a door to hide behind as the medical staff rushed in.

He waited until he could hear several of the nurses talking about the problem. He moved from his hiding spot to the reporter's room. He entered the room and stopped. Standing there was an overweight woman with a stuffed turtle. She was talking to the unconscious blond.

The portly woman greeted him. "Hi, there? I'm Wanda. I work with Becky at the newspaper. Are you a friend of Becky's?"

The man looked around. He forced himself to calm his breathing, not to panic. "No. I'm looking for my wife. I was told she was in this room."

"I'm sorry but no," Wanda said with some confusion. "This is Becky Watson's room. But if you ask someone at the nurses' station, I'm sure they can help you."

"Thank you. I'll do that." The man left and walked over to the nurses' station. A middle-aged black woman came up to assist him. He asked questions about the cafeteria and its hours. He didn't want anyone to connect him to any specific patient. He was still talking to the black woman when the middle-aged couple he saw yesterday got off the elevator and went into the blond's room. He could hear the conversation coming from the room.

"Doctor and Mrs. Watson. How nice to meet you. Of course, I wish it were under better circumstances. My name's Wanda by the way. I work with your daughter at the paper."

"Good to meet you," the father said. "We appreciate everything the paper has done for our daughter."

"Well, we love her," Wanda responded. "We're trying to arrange it so that someone from the paper is here with Becky as long as she's here. We're hoping it will give you some comfort and the chance to get some rest, go home for a shower or something. Just know that everyone at the paper is here to help you. I have the day off today, so I came by to see how she is and if you need anything from us. Also, I brought her a stuffed turtle. I thought it might bring her luck."

"How sweet," the mother replied.

The man listened to the conversation and realized he had missed his opportunity. He wouldn't be able to kill that blond girl today.

CHAPTER SIX

Keiko whined and pawed at the passenger door trying to get out of the car. "Oh, good grief Keiko," Paula said with a bit of irritation. "Let me park the car first." Keiko made a complete circle in the passenger seat and continued to stare out the car window. Paula pulled along the curb, got out, and walked around the car to open the door for Keiko, who jumped out, forcing Paula to stomp on Keiko's leash to keep her from running off.

Paula picked up the leash. She surveyed the apartment complex. The neighborhood was open to traffic coming from a major road leading to a shopping area a mile away. The lawns were well maintained, as were the two-story, brick buildings, each with four townhouse apartments. There were sidewalks and several small playgrounds with slides, monkey bars, and swings within the complex grounds. Coming up the street was the source of Keiko's yearning to get out of the car, a middle-aged woman was walking her large brown dog.

Paula waited by her car for the woman to pass, however, Keiko had a different idea. As soon as the two canines came together, they performed the ritual of sniffing and playfully pawing each other. "I'm glad they are getting along," the woman said as she held onto the leash of her pet.

"So am I," Paula replied. "It's always nice for her to meet new friends."

The woman held out her hand. "I'm Sarah Perkins. I live up the street. Are you new here?"

Paula smiled at the woman dressed in jeans and a dark blue blouse. Her brown hair had streaks of gray. "I'm Paula Stanford. And no. I'm kind of checking the place out."

"So, you're thinking of moving in. That's wonderful. This is a great place. There's a large shopping area down the road, the neighborhood is quiet, and management takes really good care of the place. They even have an emergency number for maintenance you can call 24 hours a day."

Paula monitored Keiko, ensuring the dogs were getting along. "I heard there was a shooting here yesterday."

Sarah tightened her grip on her dog's leash. "Yes, there was. It was terrible. Especially since things like that don't happen here. I didn't see it, but my neighbor, Nicole did. It was terrible, absolutely terrible. The poor child that was shot is such a sweet thing. I do hope she makes a complete recovery. Everyone here loved her."

Paula gave Sarah a look of surprise. "A child was shot. I heard it was a woman."

Sarah waved her hand at Paula. "Forgive me dear, but at my age, we tend to call everyone a child. It was a young woman, in her twenties. I won't tell you her name, to protect her privacy; but she was a lovely young lady who is simply a sweetheart. Wonderful animal lover."

"Do you know what happened?" Paula asked.

"Sorry, but no. Like I said, I didn't see it. I was there when the ambulance came, and I saw them take her away. She was alive then. Of course, everyone here is worried sick over her. The manager called someone, and they said she made it through surgery. And, of course, she's in everyone's prayers here."

"Thank you. You said your neighbor, Nicole saw it."

Sarah pulled her dog away from Keiko. The dog whined and continued to tug on its leash. "Are you a reporter?" Sarah asked with a hint of anger and apprehension in her voice as she took an in-depth look at the tall blond wearing a dark tee shirt and blue jeans.

"No," Paula answered. "The woman who was shot is Becky Watson. She's a friend of mine."

"Really," Sarah said with disbelief.

Paula pulled out her VA card and showed it to Sarah. "I'm a veteran. I just want to find out what happened to my friend. I am not a reporter, and no one here has anything to fear from me. But, please, if anyone can tell me what happened, I would really appreciate it. I just want to know what happened."

Sarah silently stared at Paula. Paula could see Sarah was thinking whether or not Paula could be trusted. Sarah's dog managed to pull closer to Keiko and Paula, who reached down and petted the dog.

"You know, I'm not that good of a judge of people," Sarah stated. "But Roscoe is. I guess if Roscoe can trust you, then I can. Wait here and I'll see if my friend will come and talk to you."

"Thank you," Paula replied.

Sarah pulled her dog away and walked back the way she had come. She stopped at a townhouse about eighty feet up the street. After a brief conversation, another woman joined Sarah as the two of them approached Paula.

The second woman of Asian descent, short, but slender, with long silver hair. Paula guessed her age to be about seventy as the woman adjusted her glasses. She was dressed in jeans and a printed blouse. "Hello," she said. "I'm Nicole. Sarah tells me you want to know what happened here yesterday."

Paula put out her hand. "I'm Paula Stanford. Becky Watson, the woman who was shot, is a friend of mine. I'm hoping someone can tell me what happened. Your friend said you saw the shooting."

Nicole shook Paula's hand. "Not quite my dear. I was outside my place putting the garbage out. You have to do that before eight o'clock. Sometimes the garbage collection is early, so you have to get it out there or you might miss it."

"I know what you mean," said Paula.

"Anyway, I was putting out my garbage when I heard two loud bangs. I didn't know what they were. But there were several of us out here. We looked around and saw that poor woman fall to the ground. Of course, everyone rushed over. The poor thing was lying on the ground, bleeding. I forget who, but one man ran and got some hand towels and put his hands over where she was bleeding. Fortunately, some people had their cell phones with them, and they called for an ambulance."

"But no one saw what happened," Paula said with disappointment.

"Sorry, but no," Nicole answered. "Until we heard the shots, no one was really paying attention to that car the person was driving."

Paula held up her hand. "Wait a minute. You saw the car?"

Nicole glanced at Sarah before returning her attention to Paula. "Well, I saw a car leave right after the woman fell down."

"What kind was it?" Paula demanded.

"I don't know. It was big and dark. Also, it was so far away. My eyes aren't good at my age." The woman again adjusted her glasses.

"Did you notice anything unusual about the car?"

"What do you mean?" Nicole asked.

"Did it have any dents, unusual marking, stickers, etc.?"

"Well, Nicole said slowly. "I did notice one thing. It's kind of silly."

"Silly can be helpful. Please."

"Well, the taillights looked like parenthesis.

"Parenthesis?"

Nicole made a motion with her hands. "Yeah, you know, those curvy lines you see in lots of math formulas. Parenthesis. I only noticed them because they were at the top of the car."

"At the top of the car?"

"Yeah, most taillights are at the bottom of the car, below the window. But these lights were at the top, next to the window."

"Did you tell the police about the taillights?"

"Oh, I couldn't. They would have thought I was silly."

Paula patted Nicole's shoulder. "Well, I don't."

CHAPTER SEVEN

In every city, there's a bar where the press hangs out. Usually, the liquor and food are cheap. In the case of Murphy's, it was the two-for-one happy hour and the free popcorn that attracted the media crowd. The fact it was located within walking distance of the newspaper also helped. The bar wasn't unique. Liquor and fried food flooded the atmosphere of the place. It had a long wooden counter serving as the main bar. Behind the bar were shelves of bottled liquor, along with a display of the different beers available. On the opposite wall, perpendicular to the wall, were four long tables, each with seating for twelve people. Just inside the door were two pool tables. In the back, behind the long tables, were several smaller tables, each with four chairs. The restrooms and kitchen were in the very back. Terry appreciated two things about Murphy's; one was the non-smoking policy, and the other was the absence of TV screens. He never understood why a bar would have eight TVs, mounted high on the walls, all with the sound turned off and each turned to a different channel.

Terry was surprised to see Paula waiting for him. He took a seat at the table she had managed to secure in the back of the room. "Good to see you," he said.

Paula grunted a greeting and took a sip from one of the two glasses in front of her. She had already finished the first one.

Terry signaled for one of the waitresses to come over. When she did, he ordered a beer. The waitress reminded him he would get two. Terry told her he would gladly accept the second one.

"Where's Keiko," Terry asked, referring to Paula's German shepherd. Since Paula rescued Keiko from a no-kill animal shelter, Paula made it a point to give the large canine lots of love and attention. Paula often brought Keiko everywhere she went so the dog would become more socialized and used to being around people.

"Left her at home," Paula replied. "I stopped by the hospital to talk to Becky's parents. Didn't want them to deal with a large dog begging for attention."

"How are they holding up?"

"Their daughter was shot, in the hospital, and there's a good chance she'll die. So how do you think they're holding up?"

"A lot better than you," Terry answered. "Why are you angry with me? I didn't do anything."

"I'm not angry with you," Paula replied. "I'm angry at the situation. Everyone expects me to have the answers. I have to take care of the situation, the parents, the dog, the plants. . ."

"Becky doesn't have a dog. And her parents live in town, so you really don't need to do anything."

"I know," Paula shouted. "But you know what the strange thing is?"

"With Becky, it would take a lot to amaze me."

Paula chuckled. "You know that twit went to high school and college here. You would think she would have a ton of friends. But no. Yeah, a lot of people know her and like her, but she really doesn't have that many friends. I'm beginning to think as sweet as she is, she's actually a lonely person."

"So are you."

"I'm a combat vet and former military police officer who is as warm and fuzzy as a cactus. Becky's different."

"Any news about who shot her?"

Paula shook her head no. "I did go over to Becky's apartment. Met a couple of her neighbors. The most useful thing one of them could tell me was the shooter's SUV's taillights looked like parenthesis. So now we've narrowed it down to a dark SUV with weird taillights. This trail is colder than an ice cream freezer."

The waitress returned with Terry's beers. Paula motioned for another round for her.

"What are you drinking?" Terry asked.

Paula answered with a single word, "whiskey." She swallowed the rest of the liquor in her glass. "And don't give me any crap about drinking too much. I get enough of that from my VA counselor."

"I don't understand why you are so angry," Terry said. "You dealt with this kind of thing when you were in the Marine Corps"

"And what makes you think I enjoyed it then. Working with families of Marines who were injured or killed. Being there in the hospital, or at the funeral. Helping families with their grief. Listening to stories about what a wonderful child the person was growing up, in high school, at church, or in scouting. It drains you. It sucks the emotions right out of you until you become a shell because that is the only way you can remain sane and still be of some assistance to the families. I had enough of it then. I don't have it in me anymore. It's hard for me to care about another human being."

Terry chuckled and took a sip of his beer.

The waitress returned and set two glasses in front of Paula. She paid the waitress, leaving her a tip. Paula waited until the waitress left. "What are you smiling at?" Paula demanded.

"You," Terry answered. "You say you can't care about people anymore, and yet here you are, angry, so angry you want to kill someone. I saw it this morning at the gym, but I thought it was just frustration. It's not. You care about Becky. You are angry because someone hurt your friend. That's right; you have a friend. Actually, more than one. But you want to make this right. You want to put the person *who shot your friend* in the hospital. Becky knows this. She knows you're her friend, and you will do anything to help her."

Paula grabbed one of the glasses in front of her and drained it in a single gulp. "Becky works with you. She's your friend. Just because I know her doesn't mean I'm her friend."

"But you like her."

Paula slammed her glass on the table. "Of course I like her. She's a nice person. But that doesn't mean I'm her friend. I just know her, that's all."

"No, it's not," Terry argued. "You like her. Becky's the kind of person everyone likes. She treats everyone with kindness. You know she wouldn't hurt anyone and she didn't deserve to get shot. That makes you angry; and you can only get that angry when a friend gets hurt for no reason."

"You're nuts."

Terry raised his mug of beer in a mock toast to Paula. "And you're right there with me."

Paula raised the second glass to Terry. "So why did you want to meet me? It can't be to tell me I'm nuts. I have counselors at the VA telling me that on a regular basis."

Terry took a USB stick out of his pocket. "I have a copy of the stories Becky worked on. I thought it might be a good idea for us to go over them and see if anything piques our interest."

"Shouldn't you have done that already and turned the information over to the police?"

"We did," Terry answered. "They took her computer from work. But Wanda, one of the reporters, and Becky's friend, made a copy of Becky's files and thinks maybe someone at the paper leaked the information to the person who shot her."

"I doubt that. If someone at the paper knew about a file on Becky's computer, they would have deleted it before you or your friend got a hold of Becky's computer."

"So, you think it's a waste to check her files?"

Paula drained her second glass. "Nope. There's a chance there's a clue in those files; but I doubt it was anyone from the paper who shot her. It's more likely it was a jilted boyfriend or some stalker."

"Crap," Terry exclaimed. "I forgot. Wanda told me about Becky's boyfriend. He's a vet over on Fourth Avenue."

"How do you know he's a veteran?"

"Not a veteran, a veterinarian. He has an office next to the Red Vine Wine Shop. We can check him out."

"I'm sure the police did that," Paula said as she stood up and gathered her things. "I'm going home. I suggest you look at the files on that flash drive. If you find anything, you can tell me tomorrow."

Paula left Terry to finish his second beer. He drank it quickly. He wanted to get home and see what the files on the flash drive would reveal.

CHAPTER EIGHT
[day three]

Freedman walked into their office and placed a file on Marshall's desk. "Autopsy report."

"Anything interesting?" he asked.

"The coroner thinks she was dead six days before anyone found her. Cause of death was two 38-caliber bullets to her chest. Since there were no shells at the scene, either the killer cleaned up his brass or used a revolver. Nothing we didn't know. I entered the ballistics report in ViCAP (Violent Criminal Apprehension Program) and NIBIN (National Integrated Ballistics Information Network). Maybe it will turn up something."

Marshall picked up the file and waved it toward Freedman. "We have a dead woman, who had a police record. According to her coworkers, she worked there for more than a decade. They say she was honest, didn't cause any trouble, and had no problems with anyone at work."

Freedman nodded his head in agreement. "When we contacted her mother, who was her next of kin, she said pretty much the same thing. She didn't have much of a social life, but she worked nights. She didn't belong to a church. She wasn't dating anyone. According to her phone records, the only people she called were restaurants that delivered food, her dentist, and a car repair shop. But there were a couple of calls to *City Times*."

"Is it possible this homicide is connected to the shooting of that young reporter a couple of days ago?

"No idea," Freedman answered. "I called the paper, but no one knew anything about her. Thought it might be her placing a personal ad in the paper, but when I talked to the advertising department, they said they never heard of her. I also checked that reporter's computer. No mention of a Tawana Williams in any of her stories."

Marshall groaned. "Great, another dead end. But check with ballistics. See if the bullets we recovered from the reporter match the ones from this homicide."

∞∞∞∞∞∞

He kept his head down. He didn't want his face to show up on any security cameras, even though they were limited to the first floor, covering the entrances and exits of the hospital. Dressed in overalls and pushing a janitorial cart, he hoped no one would notice him. His goal was to be part of the scenery, an old man who no one notices. He made it a point not to talk to anyone as he pushed a dust mop along the corridor, working his way toward his prey in the ICU.

∞∞∞∞∞∞

Terry and Diana walked past a janitor pushing a dust mop, who watched them as they made their way to Becky's room. Terry had an uneasy feeling but his concern was cut short when he and Diana found a tall, Hispanic man standing next to Becky's bed. He had an athletic build and dark hair. He was in his late twenties and fairly successful judging from his clothes.

"Hello," Diana said as they entered the room. Terry placed himself by the door to cut off any escape attempt. Diana approached Becky's bed, keeping it between her and the man. "I hate to be rude, but can I ask who you are?"

The Hispanic gentleman came over to Diana and extended his hand. "I'm Thomas Garcia. Becky's a friend. I'm just visiting to see how she's doing. May I ask who you are?"

Diana shook Thomas' hand. "I'm Diana Hawley." She gestured to Terry. "And this is Terry Lambert. We work with Becky at the newspaper. By the way, I heard you're more than a friend. Someone told me you two were dating."

Thomas chuckled. "Not quite. We went out for a couple of months, but we broke up.

"How did you know Becky was in the hospital?" Terry asked.

"The police came by my office yesterday. They told me Becky had been shot. I guess I'm a suspect because we used to date, but I can assure you I didn't shoot her."

"What can you tell us about your relationship with Becky?" Diana asked. "Look, I understand this is personal. And if it hadn't been for Becky getting shot, we would never ask. But she's a very dear friend, and we want to find out what happened."

Thomas held up his hands. "Let me stop you right there. Becky and I dated. I thought we were getting along great. But about a month ago, she became busy with a project she was working on. She was very secretive about it. All I know is she didn't have much time for me. We broke up simply because we weren't seeing that much of each other. I still like her. In fact, if she called today to get together, I would be happy. But now she's in the hospital in a coma."

"You don't know anything about this project she was working on?" Terry asked.

"Just that it took up a lot of her time. One time, I had a weekend getaway planned, but she canceled because she went to Missouri. It cost me a bundle because I was unable to get the deposit back. But what really upset me was she wouldn't tell me why she had to cancel."

"So, you were angry with her." Terry stated.

"No," Thomas answered. "I was upset by her actions, but I was never angry with her. I really liked her. I would never hurt her."

"Is there anything you can tell us about this project she was working on?" Diana asked.

"Hey, this third degree is getting to me," Thomas said, taking a few steps back. "You guys aren't cops. What's with the questions?"

"Sorry," Diana apologized. "Being reporters, we tend to ask a lot of questions. Honestly, we're just trying to find out why anyone would want to hurt Becky. About this project you mentioned. Do you know anything about it?"

Thomas took a breath to calm down. "Sorry, but no. The only thing I know about it was it had to do with something that happened a long time ago. What that was, I don't know. But maybe you can find out what it was."

Terry gave Diana a confused look. "Why would you think that?"

"She talked about a lot of old murder cases and she did leave me a flash drive. I can't access it because it needs a password. I'm hoping you guys might know the password."

"Do you know where the *City Times* office is?" Terry asked.

"Yeah."

"Bring it to us this afternoon. We'll see if we can't figure it out."

Thomas smiled. "So, what is on that flash drive is important." He reached over and patted Becky's hand. "Hope she pulls through. I would really like to see her again." Thomas nodded to Terry and Diana as he left the room.

∞∞∞∞∞

He hoped no one would notice he left the dust mop and custodial cart by the door to the stairs. He cursed growing old and how his legs and knees faltered as he rushed down the steps. He burst through the stairway door onto the first floor, breathing heavily and searching for his quarry. He pulled an inhaler of his pocket and took a couple of puffs to calm his breathing. He spotted the tall Hispanic man stepping out of the elevator. He turned away and leaned against the wall until the man walked past him. He followed the man out of the hospital.

∞∞∞∞∞

After Thomas left, a nurse came to check on Becky. "How is she doing?" Diana asked the nurse who was taking Becky's blood pressure.

"She's doing surprisingly well," the nurse answered. "She's still in a medically induced coma, but the doctors are thinking of bringing her out of it. Of course, with the pain killers, she's going to be a bit out of it, but I think in time she'll be okay."

"That's good to hear," Terry replied.

The nurse finished her task. "Listen, I know you all care about her, and that's great. Between you guys from the paper and her parents, she's getting a lot of love and caring. But right now, there really isn't anything you can do. If you leave me your information, I'll make sure you are contacted if there is any change in her condition."

Terry nodded his head in agreement. "I guess you're right." He tapped Diana on the arm. "Come on, let's get out of here and go to work."

∞∞∞∞∞∞

Thomas pulled out his keys and pushed the button to unlock his car. As he reached for the door handle, he felt a heavy blow to his head. He fell to his knees. He reached with his left hand to feel his head. Another blow landed, this time striking his hand. He fell to his right side, more out of instinct than logic. He looked over his shoulder and saw an older man in overalls standing over him. The man held a thick, wooden stick in his hand. He raised the stick to strike again.

∞∞∞∞∞∞

I really should give these things up, Francis Atlas thought to herself. As a nurse, she knew smoking cigarettes wasn't healthy, but she got hooked on them years ago in high school, when she considered smoking cool. Now it was an expensive habit that gave her a persistent cough and a greater chance for lung cancer. She snuffed the butt out in the sand-filled ash tray in the smoking area and started back to finish her shift at the hospital. She heard a thump. She looked around and saw a man with a stick getting ready to strike another person on the ground next to a car.

"Help!" She screamed. "Someone, call the police! Someone is being attacked!"

∞∞∞∞∞∞

The screams attracted his attention, as well as several others who came running out of the hospital, causing him to stop his attack on the Hispanic man. He cursed his luck. He had to leave. Both the boyfriend and that damn blond would still live. He dropped the stick, turned, and ran.

∞∞∞∞∞∞

Terry and Diana stepped out of the elevator and were greeted by several people pushing a gurney with Thomas on it. They followed the group to a bed in the emergency room. A doctor came over and began examining Thomas. A nurse pushed Terry and Diana aside and closed a curtain. While they couldn't see what was happening, they could hear the conversation.

"I'm all right," Thomas said. "Just a couple of whacks to the head, that's all."

"Yeah, still, we're going to get a couple of x-rays, just to be sure," the doctor responded. "I'm not going to release you until we're sure you're okay."

"I've got a hard head," Thomas said with a weak smile. "Still, I could use an ice pack, if you have one." A nurse pulled an instant cold pack out of a drawer, squeezed it, and handed it to Thomas.

"Want to tell us what happened?" the doctor inquired.

"No idea," Thomas answered. "I was walking to my car when someone came up and started hitting me."

"Probably a mugging," said a nurse. "Did you get a look at the person who attacked you?"

"Not really. It was some old guy in overalls. Certainly not your typical mugger."

On the other side of the curtain, Terry faced Diana. "I've got a feeling this wasn't a mugging, not by a long shot."

CHAPTER NINE

Keiko panted as Paula leaned her head against the driver's seat headrest. Keiko didn't like waiting. She could tell that Paula didn't like waiting either. Keiko wanted to get out of the car and wander around the grassy yard. This was a nice neighborhood with single-story homes, each with a wooden privacy fence surrounding the back yard, but with open front yards. A few of the homes, including the one Paula was parked in front of, had a tree in the front yard. This home also had two rose bushes in large ceramic pots flanking the front window. A car pulled into the driveway of the house where Keiko and Paula were waiting. Another car pulled behind the first one. Keiko recognized Diana and Terry as they got out of the second car. Paula got out of her car and opened the door for Keiko, who bounded over to greet Terry and Diana. Someone Keiko didn't know got out of the first car.

"Nice dog," Thomas said walking over to pet Keiko. "Whose is it?"

"Mine," Paula replied.

Diana stopped petting Keiko and waved her hand toward Thomas. "Paula, this is Thomas Garcia, Becky's boyfriend." Diana nodded toward Paula. "Thomas, this is Paula Stanford. A good friend of Becky's."

"Nice to meet you," Paula said with the obvious irritation of someone who had been waiting in a car for a while. "Is this why you wanted me to meet you here, to meet Becky's boyfriend?"

Thomas hesitatingly held up his hand. "I'm not really Becky's boyfriend. We dated for a while, but we broke up."

"Okay," Paula said slowly as she shook Thomas's hand, "Other than telling me about Becky's love life, which is none of my business, why am I here?"

"Thomas was attacked," Terry answered.

Paula stared at Terry. "Did you call the police? File a report?"

"Yes, we did all that," Terry answered. "The reason we called you is Becky gave Thomas a flash drive. We think maybe it contains information that will help us find out who shot Becky."

"It's probably the same stuff that was on the flash drive you got yesterday," Paula said.

"Could be," Terry replied, "but then, it could be something different."

Paula pulled on Keiko's leash. "Well, it won't hurt to take a look, especially since we're all here." Paula turned to Thomas. "I hope you don't mind my dog coming with us."

"Of course not," Thomas said. "I'm a vet, a veterinarian."

Thomas opened the door to his home and invited everyone in. While his computer was warming up, he brought out soft drinks for everyone and a bowl of water for Keiko. The computer was a laptop set on a small table in the living room. The room had a cream-colored carpet, a couch, two armchairs, a coffee table, and a long wooden, two-shelved bookcase with the television set on top. On the wall were three Salvador Dali prints. Paula looked at the surrealistic paintings and wondered why people thought these paintings were art and yet they tended to call her mentally unbalanced.

Thomas inserted the flash drive into the computer. It demanded a password. "This is what I was hoping you could help me with. I can't figure out what the password could be."

While Terry and Diana looked over Thomas's shoulder, Paula remained on the couch. "You know the password," Paula said as she took a drink from her glass.

"No, I don't," Thomas responded. "Becky gave me the drive, but not the password."

Paula took a deep breath. "The password is something that only you two would know. Some kind of inside joke or special phrase you always use."

Thomas was silent for a moment. "Nothing comes to mind."

"How did you two meet?" Paula asked.

"You're not going to believe this," Thomas said with a chuckle.

"It's Becky, I'll believe anything," Paula answered.

Thomas blushed. He got up, went over to his closet and pulled out a huntsman hat. "We met at a Sherlock Holmes event at a local bar. It turns out we're both avid Sherlock Holmes fans."

"That's it," Terry exclaimed. "Try Sherlock Holmes as the password."

Thomas returned to the computer and typed in the name. The computer still demanded a password.

"Try Doctor Watson," Diana said with a hint of doubt in her voice.

Once again Thomas typed in the name and the computer demanded a password.

"Maybe it's the housekeeper's name," Terry suggested. "I can't remember her name, but we can look it up."

"How about where you and Becky first met?" Paula suggested.

"That's the Holmes Pub," Thomas replied. "That's because it's on Baker Street. Can you believe it, there is a street named Baker Street in Fort Stebbins?"

Terry snapped his fingers. "That's it. Try 2-2-1-B Baker Street."

Thomas typed in the address. The file opened up. "How did you know?" he asked. Terry gave Thomas a smug look. "It's elementary my dear Watson. Actually, I remember Wanda telling the detectives it was her password for her computer at work."

Paula glared at Terry. "Forget about Terry playing Sherlock Holmes. What do you have on the flash drive?"

"Quite a few files here," Diana answered. "They are women. I don't remember any of these as stories she was working on."

"Wait a minute," Terry demanded as he started typing more words onto his cell phone.

Everyone in the room remained silent, waiting for enlightenment from Terry. "Yeah, I thought so," he said showing his cell phone to the other in the room. "All the names; Mrs. Hudson, Irena Adler, Elsie Patrick; they are all names of women in Sherlock Holmes novels."

Thomas clicked on the file labeled Mrs. Hudson. It opened to a police report about the murder of a young lady named Marianne Kesler. The murder occurred thirty-four years ago.

"I remember this case," Terry said. "The police department sent her DNA to Lineage DNA, and they identified her. She was known as the

Sunshine Girl because of the Florida tee shirt she was wearing when her body was discovered. We did an article on her a few months ago."

Thomas closed that file and clicked on another file labeled Irena Adler. It opened to another homicide case, Denise Varney. He moved the cursor to the third file. Again, a homicide case appeared, as did the fourth one he clicked on. "These are all murders. Why was she investigating all these murders?"

"What are the dates on them?" Paula asked.

"Well, none of them are recent," Thomas replied. "All of them happened years ago."

"So, she was investigating cold cases," Paula stated. "Now we have to find out why these cold cases are so important?"

"What makes you think they're important?" Thomas asked.

Paula stood up and grabbed Keiko's leash. "Because someone doesn't want Becky to find out who committed those murders. That's why she was shot, and why you were attacked."

Thomas looked at everyone in the room. "So, what do we do?"

"We go to the police," Terry answered.

CHAPTER TEN

"Oh, good grief," Marshall groaned as he entered the squad room and saw four individuals and a dog waiting for him. Freedman followed Marshall into the room and immediately went over to pet the dog.

"Hey, you brought your dog," Freedman said to Paula.

Paula glared at Freedman. "I'm amazed at how observant you are," she said sarcastically.

The squad room resembled a standard classroom. There were forty chairs with attached writing tables arranged in five rows of eight. A lectern and magnetic white board were at the front of the room, with a cork bulletin board covered with fliers on each side of the white board. Marshall sat down in a chair next to Paula. Freedman took the chair next to Marshall.

"Happy to see us?" Paula asked.

"Overjoyed," Marshall replied. "And I thought it would be another boring day of muggings, assaults, and homicides."

Paula leaned forward and grinned. "So happy to be of service."

Thomas cleared his throat. "I hope there isn't a problem." He stuck out his hand to Marshall. "We met yesterday. You came by my office to ask me about Becky."

Marshall shook Thomas's hand. "Yes, I remember. So, what brings all of you in here today?"

Terry, Diana, and Thomas looked to Paula. "Why are you staring at me?" she demanded. "Give him the flash drive."

"What's this?" Marshall asked.

Paula pointed to the flash drive. "That's the reason Becky was shot."

∞∞∞∞∞∞

"Why do you have this?" Marshall asked. "This is a police investigation. You're not supposed to be involved."

Thom raised his hand.

"This isn't high school," Marshall retorted with some frustration. "You don't need to raise your hand to talk."

Thom nodded. "Becky left me the flash drive in case something happened. I guess it was her insurance."

Marshall stared at the flash drive. "Why didn't you tell us about this yesterday when we talked to you?"

"I forgot I had it," Thom replied sheepishly. "Besides, I didn't really know how to access it until I ran into Becky's friends."

Freedman brought in a laptop computer. Within minutes he had the files on the flash drive open. He clicked on the first one which was about Marianne Kesler.

"What do you know about the case known as *The Sunshine Girl?*" Marshall asked.

Diana and Terry looked at each other. Diana spoke up. "We ran a story about it a couple of months ago. She was a Jane Doe until your department sent a sample of her DNA to Lineage DNA. They were able to identify her using the same DNA testing used in ancestry DNA testing, the kind you see on TV. According to a statement issued by your department, you were able to confirm her identity through DNA testing of a sister who lives in Missouri."

"That's it?" Freedman inquired.

"So far, that's it," Diana answered.

"Since you've brought in the drive, then let me fill you in," Marshall said. "The victim's name is Marianne Kesler, age nineteen. She was known to be a free spirit, a polite way of saying she was homeless and sexually promiscuous. While we know she traveled around because forensic evidence showed traces of plants and soil from other geographical areas, specifically, Florida. Then of course, there was the tee shirt. We think she might have been down there for Spring Break before coming up here. We have no idea why she was here. We believe she was hitchhiking through the area, got picked up, and the driver killed her."

"So, she remained a Jane Doe and no one cared," Paula said not trying to hide the disappointment she felt.

"Not quite," Marshall replied. "Someone opened this and several other cold cases. Back to Ms. Kesler. Autopsy revealed she had been beaten but cause of death was strangulation. Not only did she have bruises on her face and upper body, but she also had a lacerated liver, which meant she fell to the floor and was kicked repeatedly. Postmortem lividity, also known as livor mortis, shows she was seated in a car or a chair for a while before her body was dumped in a ditch on the side of Snyder Road, a rural road without any kind of lighting. She was wrapped in military olive drab poncho, which helped hide her. Her body was discovered about a day and a half after she was killed. There was no identification on the body, hence the labeling her a Jane Doe. Also, her shoes were missing, which led us to believe she was killed in a room. It looks like someone expected to have sex with her, she refused, and he beat her to death."

"What about her personal effects?" Paula asked.

Marshall picked up a list from the file. "Her personal effects included a Florida sunshine tee shirt, blue jeans, underwear and a bra, forty-three cents in change, some Juicy Fruit chewing gum, a matchbook from a convenience store and gas station on Bradley Road, along with a receipt from that store for Chap Stick, a pack of cigarettes, and nail clippers."

"What about fingerprints and DNA?" Terry inquired.

"We found a partial print on the matchbook, which was hers, some DNA evidence. But there wasn't a match in any database," Marshall answered.

"Excuse me," Diana interjected. "Why did you send this woman's DNA to this lab now? This murder happened more than thirty years ago. Why reopen it now?"

Marshall chuckled. "For that, you need to ask the Professor."

Diana squinted her eyes. "The Professor?"

"Detective Jennifer Gunn," Freedman responded.

∞∞∞∞∞∞

Marshall made a phone call. Twenty minutes later, an attractive woman in her late thirties came in accompanied by a man of Asian descent. The woman was holding several folders in her arms.

Freedman greeted the two of them. "Professor, how nice to see you."

"Don't call me that," the woman replied. She was dressed in jeans, a tan police polo shirt with her name and a badge embroidered on it. She had short dark hair and dark eyes, as well as an authoritative voice. "I am Detective Jennifer Gunn."

Freedman held up his hands, "Professor, don't you ever smile?"

"The closest I've seen her to a smile is after she's had about four shots of bourbon," the Asian man said. He looked to be about the same age as the woman. He was wearing chinos and a dark blue shirt which accented his black hair and slim build. He walked up to Paula and stuck out her hand. "I'm Detective Steven Oha."

Gunn pointed to the others in the room. "Who are they? What's with the dog?"

"The dog is with me," Paula answered as she shook Oha's hand. "I'm Paula Stanford."

Gunn stared at Paula for a few seconds. "You served, didn't you? I can always recognize another veteran."

"Yeah, I did," Paula admitted, "Marine Corps, Iraq, got out five years ago."

Gunn nodded. "Army. I also pulled a couple of tours in Iraq."

Paula pointed to Terry and Diana. "This is Terry and that's Diana. They work at *City Times*. A couple of days ago, a friend of ours was shot in front of her apartment. The other gentleman is Thomas Garcia. He's also a friend of the woman who was shot. We were hoping you could tell us something about some cold cases that might lead to the person who shot her."

"A young blond woman," Gunn asked. "I remember her. She was interested in several of our cold cases."

"Why?" Diana inquired.

"She was researching all the cold cases, looking for certain ones that fit a pattern. She asked a lot of questions about some of the cases, but the ones she was interested in are all connected. We believe they were committed by the same killer."

"Let's back it up for a minute," Paula interjected. "There's one case in particular, the Jane Doe case you labeled as *The Sunshine Girl*. Do you know why she was so interested in that case?"

"Nope," was Gunn's answer. "I assumed it was because the victim was so young."

"Let me ask you another question," Paula said. "Why did you send this person's DNA off to be tested now. You could have sent it off thirty years ago."

"No, I couldn't," Gunn replied. "Thirty years ago, they didn't have the technology they have today. I read about this new company wanting to help identify John and Jane Does. So, I sent a sample off to them. They came back with the results. I was able to contact a sister and through DNA testing we were able to confirm the victim was Marianne Kesler."

"Do you have any leads on that case now?" Terry asked.

"Nothing I'm going to tell the press," Gunn answered. "These cases are still active. We need to be careful about what information we release to the public."

"Mellow out Professor," Freedman said.

"I told you don't call me that," Gunn barked.

Thomas looked over to the woman. "Just how did you get that nickname?"

"Are you kidding?" Oha replied. "Detective Gunn here is famous. She has a PhD in criminal justice and has written several books on criminal investigation. She's always being asked to talk at conferences and universities."

"Hey. I'm a cop. Just because I have some fancy degree doesn't mean I'm better than anyone else."

"I know how you feel," Terry replied. "People tend to notice how you're different instead of how you're the same as them."

Gunn smiled at Terry. "Something tells me you're dealt with that issue quite a bit."

"Yeah," Terry answered.

"Sorry to interrupt, but maybe you could tell us about the other cold cases?" Paula asked.

Gunn set several folders down on the table. "Marshall told me you were interested in the cases that the reporter was investigating. As I said, these cases are still open. Anything we tell you, stays here. It's not for public distribution. We believe the killer is the same for all of them. The second victim was listed as Jane Doe, but we were able to identify her within a few days by comparing dental charts between the victim and missing persons' reports. Her name was Denise Varney. She was also beaten and strangled. Her body was wrapped in a brown tarp and dumped in a ditch on a rural road with almost no illumination. The third victim, Theresa Hallman, the same; beaten, strangled, body dumped in a ditch on a poorly lit road."

"Was there any evidence; anything to lead to a killer?" Terry asked.

"For the *Sunshine Girl*, we did find some DNA evidence, but no hits on any data banks. On Denise Varney, we found another partial print and delivery company matchbook. We think it belonged to the killer; there were no matching prints from the victim. We also found a receipt from a convenience store/gas station. It was the same place as *The Sunshine Girl*. Also, we have DNA evidence from a few of the other cases, possibly the killer's since they match an DNA sample taken from *The Sunshine Girl*."

Diana took a few minutes to look at the files and crime scene photos. "And the police are still investigating these cases, even after all these years?"

"These cases were never closed," Gunn answered. "I make it a point to pull them out at least once a year and see if we can do anything new. I read about Lineage DNA. That's why I sent them the *Sunshine Girl's* DNA. Even if I can't solve the case, it can provide some closure for families to know what happened to their missing loved ones."

"Okay, let me make sure I've got this right," Paula said. "Becky comes down here and begins checking out these cold cases. Then she gets shot. It seems to me she uncovered something about them. Are these the only cold cases you have?"

"Of course not," Gunn replied. "But these are the ones your friend was interested in, and the ones with an obvious connection. We also went through ViCAP. But you will notice that many of these crimes occurred more than twenty years ago, before ViCAP was available to all police departments. That means there are crimes out there we don't know about, although some departments are going back and entering their cold cases."

"But we're lucky," Oha added. "A couple of homicides are from Park Hills, which is just up the road from us, were listed in ViCAP. They sent us copies of their files that fit our profile. So far, we have uncovered five murders similar to *The Sunshine Girl*."

Terry sighed. "That means you have a serial killer."

"No," Gunn replied. "It means we have a serial killer who has remained undetected and hidden for more than thirty years. He's grown old, learned new tricks, but is just as deadly as he was when he first started. It's that discovery that got your friend shot."

"Why do you say that?" Thomas asked.

"We got the ballistics report back," Freedman answered. "The same gun was used in the attack on your friend and in a homicide that took place a week ago. There's no doubt about it. The killer is after your friend."

∞∞∞∞∞∞

Thomas said goodbye and left. Terry and Diana returned to their office, but Keiko enjoyed the next several hours. While Paula, along with Gunn and Oha, examined the files on the cold cases, several of the police officers came up to give Keiko treats and two of them took her out for a walk around the station. Many others stopped to pet or to snuggle with her. "Don't get used to it," Paula warned the dog. "As soon as I finish here, we're going home."

Paula noted both Marianne Kesler and Denise Varney visited the same convenience store/gas station, located on Bradley Road, less than a quarter mile from Highway 431. There were recordings of the two victims' visits. In both cases, the women entered the store alone, on foot, and made small purchases. The recordings showed Marianne with a backpack from which she pulled a wallet to pay for her purchases. Denise had a purse with a shoulder strap. Marianne purchased Chap Stick and cigarettes. Denise bought a soda and cigarettes. The recordings showed the women leaving the store, alone, and walking away toward the interstate. Paula noted that neither Marianne's backpack nor Denise's purse were listed among the victim's belongings. In both cases, the personal effects were limited to the victim's clothes and whatever was in their pockets. She noticed this pattern was the same for all the victims. Paula watched the videos several times to see if any other people or vehicles appeared in both videos. The only person to appear in both videos was the shop owner, but he never left the store.

∞∞∞∞∞

Diana was worried about Terry. During the entire drive back from the police station, he didn't say a single word. They stepped out of the elevator together. Several people in the office greeted them, but Terry failed to notice them. He sat down at his computer, turned it on, and stared at it for several minutes. Then he started typing.

A few days ago, one of our reporters was shot in front of her apartment. This wasn't some random shooting of a person being in the wrong place at the wrong time. This was a deliberate attempt to stop the press, the voice and protector of our civil rights, from informing the public about a murderer in our mists. The first homicide we know of occurred more than thirty years ago when an unidentified young woman was brutally beaten and strangled to death, then left in a ditch. Known at that time as the Sunshine Girl, she was recently identified as Marianne Kesler. She was murdered on May 16th, 1986. Four years later, another woman, Denise Varney, age 22, a prostitute was beaten and strangled. She too was dumped in a ditch after being killed on April 23rd, 1990.

The last known victim of this murderer was Theresa Hallman, age 24, a waitress and mother of a two-year-old. Her life was taken from her on March 5th, 2003. Two of these women were last seen in the early evening hours in the area of a combined convenience store and gas station on Bradley Road. It is now time for us to step up and do what we can to bring this criminal to justice. Anyone with any information about any of these cases, no matter how insignificant one may think, should notify Detective Jennifer Gunn of the Fort Stebbins Police Department at jgunn@fstpd.org or 508-228-XXXX.

Terry made sure his name was in the byline. He wanted the killer to know who was after him.

CHAPTER ELEVEN
[day four]

Terry groaned as he stepped out of the elevator the next morning. He was sore from his exercise session the other day. He trudged over to his workstation and pulled out his chair. Set on the seat was a dull red whoopee cushion. Terry looked around and noticed Ashford looking down at his desk, trying to hide a smirk.

Terry picked up the whoopee cushion and walked over to Ashford's desk. "Really? A whoopee cushion? Did you really think I would fall for it?"

Ashford chuckled. "You never know. The oldies are goodies."

"Yeah, right," Terry replied as he pointed to nozzle of the cushion at Ashford. Terry grabbed the cushion with both hands.

"No!" Ashford shouted as Terry squeezed the cushion. Before Terry could react, a stream of shaving cream came out squirting. Ashford stood up, covered with shaving cream, groaning, while the rest of the editorial staff laughed, silently applauding the fact Ashford's prank had backfired, making him the victim.

Terry was giggling, still holding the cushion aimed at Ashford. "Whoops," he said. "I didn't know it was loaded. But you're right. The oldies are goodies. Great gag."

Ashford grabbed some leftover napkins from his morning coffee and wiped the shaving cream off his face. "I'll get you for this," he hissed.

Terry tossed the deflated whoopee cushion on Ashford's desk. "Hey, it was your gag. It just hit the wrong target. Not my fault." Terry was smiling as he returned to his desk.

∞∞∞∞∞∞

"Behave yourself," Paula demanded of Keiko. Keiko stared up at Paula and followed her down the corridor of the hospital. The nurse greeted them as they entered Becky's room. "Well, who do we have here?"

"This is Keiko?" Paula replied. "I know I shouldn't bring a dog into the room, but I couldn't leave her in the car. Besides, I've seen other dogs in here, so I didn't think there would be a problem."

"We do allow therapy dogs. They do wonders for the patients. And being an animal lover myself, I can understand not leaving your dog in the car. As long as she doesn't cause any trouble, I don't think anyone will really say anything."

Paula reached down and petted Keiko. "Thanks. How is Becky doing?"

The nurse tossed her stethoscope around her neck. "She's holding her own. Her vital signs are good, there doesn't seem to be any complications from the surgery. It will take time, but I'm sure she'll be all right."

Paula sat on the bed next to Becky. Keiko put her front paws on the bed and nuzzled the unconscious patient as a sign of comfort. "Thanks," Paula said to the nurse. "I think I'll stay with her for a while, at least until her parents come in."

"That's fine dear. Stay as long as. . ." The nurse didn't get to finish. A police officer entered the room.

"Need to see some identification," the officer demanded.

The nurse showed him her hospital ID. Paula pulled out her driver's license. "What's the problem?" Paula asked.

"Just need to check everyone's ID," he answered. "Can you tell me why you're here?" Paula noticed the officer was copying her information in his notebook.

"I'm visiting my friend," Paula stated, motioning to Becky laying in the hospital bed.

The officer handed Paula back her license. "Have you been here before?"

"Yes, I have," Paula answered. "If you need to confirm, you can ask Detective Marshall or Detective Freedman. They know me and my friend, who was shot four days ago."

"Yeah, I heard about that," the officer acknowledged. "Thanks for your cooperation." The officer waved his notebook as a sign of goodbye and left the room.

"Oh, my goodness," the nurse exclaimed. "I wonder what happened."

"Nothing good," Paula replied. "Nothing good at all."

∞∞∞∞∞∞

He noticed the hospital security had set up a table and had everyone show some form of identification and sign in. He didn't want his name on any paperwork. He left and walked around to the emergency room, hoping to get in without having to sign in. If he pretended to be looking for someone who had been brought in by ambulance, he should be able to get past the reception desk. He took out his cell phone and acted like he was having a conversation as he waited. Luck was with him. Less than five minutes later an ambulance pulled up and took a woman into the ER. He waited for another few minutes before going in.

∞∞∞∞∞∞

"Terry, can you come here," Diana called to Terry as he was returning from getting a cup of coffee.

Terry walked over her desk as Diana brought up Lineage DNA on her computer. A couple of clicks with her mouse and several photographs of Marianne Kesler appeared.

She was an attractive teenage girl with long, reddish-brown hair and dark brown eyes. She had a beautiful smile in one photograph showing her enjoying the butterflies in an open field. "She's a pretty young lady," Terry said. "It's a shame someone ended her life at such a young age.

Think about it, if she hadn't been killed, what would she be today? She could be a woman with a successful career. Or a mother with grown children. She would be looking forward to having grandchildren to spoil."

"Yeah, yeah, you're right. A real home on the prairie kind of gal. Look at the photographs. Do you notice anything?"

"She's happy," Terry answered.

"Look who posted them."

Terry saw the photos were posted by a Glenn Doty "So?" he asked.

"Let me ask you this. Do you have any photographs of your old girlfriends?"

"No, not really. I have several of Kristen, actually quite a few. But maybe the person who posted these is a relative."

"I doubt it," Diana replied. "As for photos of Kristen, that doesn't count. You were married to her. Of course, you have lots of pictures of her. You were in love with her."

"And your point is?"

"My point is," Diana stated, "whoever posted these pictures has kept them for thirty years. That person was in love with Marianne."

∞∞∞∞∞∞

The man ran into the emergency room and demanded to know where was the woman the paramedics had brought in ten minutes earlier. Before the person behind the counter could answer, he rushed over to the treatment areas in the ER. A nurse came over and led him back to the receptionist. She explained he needed to fill in a form. He pushed her away and ran down the hall, looking into each treatment area behind the curtains. A nurse came out of the treatment area and tried to calm him. He asked about the woman that was brought in. The nurse told him she was taken to the operating room on the sixth floor. He thanked her and ran through the door leading into the hospital. He got on the elevator. He had done it. He had gotten in without being identified. Now he could kill that young blond woman.

∞∞∞∞∞

Diana smiled at the police officer behind the Plexiglas shield with small holes at face level for people to speak through and a small depression at the bottom for passing documents. "Is it possible to see Detectives Marshall and Freedman?" she asked.

The patrol officer stared at the attractive brunette and the short man with her before picking up the phone and informing the detectives they had visitors. A few minutes later Freedman opened one of the doors leading out of the foyer into the bowels of the police station.

Diana smiled at Freedman. "We have some great news for you." Terry stood next to Diana and silently waved to Freedman.

"You have tickets to the playoffs, and you're willing to share them?"

Diana crossed her arms. Freedman could tell she wasn't amused. "Okay," he said. "What have you got for me?"

"A clue, a lead, the killer," Diana answered.

Freedman motioned for Diana and Terry to enter. "Looking forward to hearing this, especially since you solved a case that we haven't managed to close in more than thirty years."

"In a way, it was Marianne herself who lead us to her killer," Terry replied. "If you can take us to a computer, I can show you."

Freedman led Terry and Diana upstairs to Detective Gunn's office. It was furnished with two office cubicles, one for Detective Gunn and the other for Detective Oha. Lining two of the walls were shelves filled with boxes, books, and files. In the center of the room was a very large conference table. Detective Gunn was standing over several open files on the conference table. Opposite her was Detective Oha.

"Professor, got a guest for you," Freedman called out.

"Don't call me that," the woman commanded.

"Okay, okay," Freedman said chuckling. "Still, there's someone here to see you."

"Hey," Terry said with a wave of his hand. "We met yesterday. I'm Terry Lambert and this is Diana Hawley. We work with Becky Watson.

She was shot a few days ago and before that she talked to you about some cold cases."

"Yeah, I remember you. And call me Jennifer. So, what can I do for you?"

Diana stepped forward. "We were doing some research on one of the cases. We think we might have come up with a lead or at least a suspect for that case."

"What are you doing getting involved in an active investigation?" Jennifer demanded.

Terry cleared his throat. "We were just looking at information on the internet. We think we found something."

"Which case?" Jennifer asked.

"The murder of Marianne Kesler."

"What have you got?"

"Have you checked out the Lineage DNA website?" Diana asked. "I was looking at it earlier today and noticed there are several photographs of Marianne on that site. Have you wondered where they came from?"

Jennifer folded her arms across her chest. "Yes, we checked on who posted the photographs. It was an old boyfriend, Glenn Doty. He had a high school crush on her."

"Yes, Diana gleefully shouted. "So, he's a suspect. I just broke this case wide open for you."

"You get to tell him," Jennifer said to Oha.

Oha motioned for Terry and Diana to sit down. "No, he's not a suspect. He was in the Army, stationed in Germany at the time. And yes, we did check to make sure he hadn't come back on leave. He spent a year there and didn't come home for leave the entire time. Also, he moved out to Oregon about twenty-five years ago for a job with the government. I doubt he would keep coming back here to commit the other homicides."

"Crap, feel kind of foolish," Terry sheepishly said. "I was kind of hoping we had something useful for you."

Jennifer placed her hand on Terry's shoulder. "Hey, don't beat yourself up over this. It was a good hunch. It showed you're thinking along the right track. Just because we did it first doesn't mean it was wrong to ask us to check it out. In fact, we want you to come to us if you have any ideas or leads about who might have killed these women or shot your coworker. We like it when people work with us, when they tell us about unusual events or people. If they didn't, we wouldn't be able to solve most crimes. But, and I mean a very big but, don't take any risks. Be eyes and ears only. Don't try to be a hero. If you have anything, come to us."

"It's a pity the pictures are a dead end. Can you tell me anything about the case?" Terry pleaded.

"Sure. The boyfriend didn't do it."

∞∞∞∞∞∞

He made his way to the ICU where his prey was located. He grabbed a pamphlet from a display stand and pretended to look at it as he walked down the hallway. He took a quick look to ensure no one was watching. He entered the room.

A tall woman with a large German shepherd dog stared at him as he entered. She was the same woman he saw that day in waiting room at the ER. "Afternoon," the woman said. "Do you need something?"

The woman didn't move. The hair on the dog's back started to stand up. "Can I help you?" the woman said as she stepped around the patient's bed and placed herself between him and the patient.

"I was looking for my wife," he replied.

The woman took a step toward him. "Then let me get the nurse to help you find whoever you are looking for."

"That's okay," he said. "I'll check with them myself and find out where she is." The individual quickly left the room. *Damn it*, he thought, *it's getting really hard to kill that girl.*

CHAPTER TWELVE

That evening, Paula was seated at a table with Diana, Terry, and Wanda. "One of the few things I love about Murphy's is happy hour," Paula stated as she downed her first glass of Jack Daniels.

"You love the two for the price of one," Diana replied, sipping her cocktail.

Paula stared at the empty glass in her hand. *Dammit it,* she thought, *that damn VA counselor is haunting me.*

Wanda was looking over the menu. "Do they have anything good here? It seems everything is burgers, sandwiches, and fries."

"It's a bar," Paula answered. "The only thing you'll get here is pub grub." Paula set her empty glass on the table.

"And popcorn," Terry added, munching on a fistful while drinking a beer.

Wanda put down the menu. "Oh, never mind about the food. What are we going to do? We must do something. Becky was shot investigating these murders. Do you think there's a serial killer out there, stalking poor defenseless women?"

Terry, Diana, and Wanda looked at Paula. Their staring made her uncomfortable. Even Keiko stared at Paula from the floor. "Good grief," Paula exclaimed. "Why are you looking at me?"

"We need to do something," Wanda pleaded. "There's a killer out there. He could be after one of us next."

"I don't think so," Terry interjected. "Detectives Marshall and Freedman were surprised by these cases, mainly because they happened many years ago. I don't think there's anything we need to worry about."

"Then why was Becky shot?" Paula said. "She was looking into these cases. She found something that frightened the killer. She found a clue to the killer's identity. And until he is caught, her life is in danger. And don't forget about the attack on Becky's boyfriend."

"Maybe we should go and guard her," Wanda said. "Maybe the killer will try again, this time when she's helpless in the hospital."

"I doubt that," Paula said to reassure everyone. Even as she said it, the incident with the strange man coming into Becky's room at the ICU gave her concern. "First, there are nurses and security to get pass. Second, there are her parents, who are practically living there. Also, Terry told me someone from the paper is usually there with the parents. That's too many people and too many chances at getting caught to try anything."

Wanda leaned forward and spoke in a muffled voice. "Couldn't he sneak in late at night, when no one is there and do something?"

"You still have the nurses and security," Paula replied. "Don't forget, Becky's in ICU where she is under constant observation. Besides, late at night, all visitors are noticed. That is something he doesn't want."

"So, we do nothing," Diana inquired.

"Of course, we do something," Paula answered. "You three work at the newspaper. Do some research and see what you can find out."

"We don't know anything about any of the cases," Diana said with some frustration in her voice.

"We'll start where Becky started," Terry stated. "We know the case that started this all was that cold case about the *Sunshine Girl* some thirty years ago. We ran a story about it a couple of months ago."

"That's one case," Diana said. "What about the others. There were several cases on that flash drive."

"Becky's a relatively inexperienced reporter," Terry continued. "If she could find other leads, so can we." Terry pointed to Wanda. "You find out things about everyone in this town, all their secrets. And Diana has quite a bit of investigative reporting experience. As for me, no one is better at going through old files and finding details than me. Why, we're unstoppable."

Paula finished her second whiskey and signaled for the waitress to bring her two more. *So, what if I like to drink? What's the harm in that?*

"Well, since you all have superpowers, that means Keiko and I can take the night off and relax."

Diana raised her drink to all at the table. "To us, to solving the crimes. . ."

Wanda raised her glass. "And to keeping Becky safe."

CHAPTER THIRTEEN
[day five]

Experience had taught him well. Many people were afraid to sneak into any place open twenty-four hours a day, but he knew it was easy. He knew the hospital staff changed shifts at six, and early morning was always the best time. The staff would be more interested in getting their coffee than checking on visitors. This held true for the security team. He only had to wait until they were distracted and he easily slipped by them. Besides, he was wearing the shirt and pants medical staff called scrubs. Carrying a clipboard, pretending to check some records, he was practically invisible. Yes, the staff would see him, but no one would notice him. All he had to do was wait for the right moment when no one was in that young lady's room.

∞∞∞∞∞∞

People don't understand dogs. Dog owners claim they do, but their furry friends always find ways to surprise them. Fortunately, dogs understand people. It was no surprise to Keiko that her owner, Paula, was up at four in the morning. Keiko had given up on having any kind of routine with this woman. Keiko knew Paula rarely slept more than a few hours. Her owner often woke up because of nightmares or would spend hours in front of the TV drinking alcohol before finally falling asleep in the early hours of the morning. Wanda's fear for Becky's safety haunted Paula throughout the night. Today, Paula was up at four o'clock. Keiko knew it meant they were going somewhere.

Keiko enjoyed this time. It was just the two of them and that meant she could ride in the front seat with Paula. The car pulled into the parking lot of the hospital. Entering the building, Keiko was overwhelmed with smells she didn't like and noises that bothered her. Paula took a moment to kneel down and comfort the dog. "Relax," Paula said. "There's nothing to be afraid of. No one is going to do anything to you."

Paula stopped to talk to a security guard who allowed her and Keiko to pass. After showing him her driver's license, he informed Paula the cafeteria was open, and the coffee was fresh. Paula started in one direction but changed her mind and went to the cafeteria. She got herself a large coffee and a muffin. Keiko was disappointed to discover the food was not for her.

They left the cafeteria. On their way to ICU, they passed several doctors, nurses, and other medical personnel. They walked past one person in scrubs carrying a clipboard. Keiko didn't like that man.

∞∞∞∞∞∞

He kept an eye on the door to the room where his quarry was. The tall woman that he met yesterday with her dog walked past him. The woman barely noticed him; probably because he was wearing scrubs instead of street clothes; but the dog watched him as they passed. It was as if the dog was saying *I see you*. The tall woman stopped at the nurses' station. The dog continued to stare at him. A nurse came up to the woman and led her into the room where his prey slept. After a few minutes, he walked past the room, looked in, and saw the woman and dog sitting there, guarding his target. Once again, that nosy, young blond would get to live a little longer.

∞∞∞∞∞∞

The hospital came alive as more nurses and doctors arrived and started their shifts. Family and friends came in to visit those staying in the hospital. Through all this hustle and bustle, even after drinking a large coffee, somehow Paula fell asleep in the chair next to Becky's bed. Keiko quietly watched each person who passed by. She stood up and pulled on her leash, waking Paula, when a nurse came to check on Becky.

"Good morning," the nurse said as she checked on Becky. "What brings you in this early?"

Paula took a sip of her coffee and made an ugly face. She hated cold coffee. She stood up and stretched, then pointed to Becky. "Couldn't sleep, well actually, woke up early. Thought it would be a good idea to come and keep her company, just in case she woke up."

"So, you work at the newspaper too," the nurse commented.

"No, I'm just a friend," Paula answered.

The nurse finished checking everything and inputted the information into a handheld computer. "I think it's great her friends and coworkers come to visit. There's always someone here and I know her parents appreciate it. So, you go right on doing what you're doing."

Paula smiled and nodded thanks.

"Also, if you don't mind," the nurse said in a quiet voice, "I'll see if I can't find some leftovers on the breakfast trays for your dog. You would be surprised at how many of our patients refuse to eat the bacon."

"Thanks," Paula said petting Keiko. "I'm sure she'll appreciate it."

The nurse left the room with Keiko wagging her tail. Somehow, she knew she was in for a treat.

∞∞∞∞∞∞

"Oh, my goodness," Lynda exclaimed as she entered with a gentleman. "What a beautiful dog." She came over and started petting Keiko.

"Her name is Keiko," Paula stated. "Good to see you again."

"Have you been here all night?" the man asked.

"No," Paula answered. "I have trouble sleeping, so I came in early to visit. The staff let Keiko come in. I guess they think it's therapeutic."

"How's she doing?" Lynda asked.

"Okay, I guess," said Paula. "A nurse checked on her a while ago and she seemed all right."

Becky's mother walked over and took Becky's hand. Paula picked up Keiko's leash and walked toward the door.

"Will you be coming back?" Lynda asked.

Paula stopped at the door and turned to face Lynda. "Right now, I think I'll go home and try to get some sleep. But I'll be back. It's a Marine thing. We never leave a friend behind." Paula smiled and left.

∞∞∞∞∞

Later that day, Paula was sitting on her couch with her feet up on an old footlocker, which she used as her coffee table. Paula stared at the tumbler with two fingers of Jack Daniels in it. Keiko with her head on Paula's thigh looked up at her owner.

"Wasted days and wasted nights," Paula said in a sing-song voice as she petted Keiko. "That's what it was today. Let's take stock of our accomplishments. We went to the hospital, where I fell asleep next to a comatose patient. Went to the gym, where I worked out, all by myself. And now we are at home, trying to figure out how Becky discovered there was a serial killer out there, and why her boyfriend was attacked in the hospital parking lot."

Paula held the glass up to the light, examining the amber liquid. "Do you think the VA counselor is right?" Paula said to the glass. "Am I becoming a drunk, an alcoholic, a basket case needing booze and drugs to get to sleep?"

Paula looked down at Keiko. "The hell with it," she said as she downed the whiskey in a single gulp.

CHAPTER FOURTEEN
[day six]

Even though Le Rue had the best and most expensive pastries and coffee, Paula liked the place and enjoyed starting her morning here. It was close to the gym where she worked, there were free refills on coffee, she could bring Keiko here if she sat outside, and they had free papers for their customers. Paula read Terry's editorial. *Dumb*, she thought. *The killer shot Becky because he thought she was getting too close. He certainly wouldn't stop at shooting a dwarf threatening him.* Paula hoped Terry would come into the gym today for more self-defense lessons when she was working out. She would need to teach him to keep a low profile and out of the enemy's sights.

"Hey there, how are you doing today?"

Paula looked up and saw Ashford standing on the other side of the iron railing separating the sidewalk café from pedestrian traffic. "So far, so good," Paula answered. "What are you up to today?"

Ashford spread his arms out and smiled. "I'm enjoying the sunshine, greeting the world, and bringing hope and happiness to the masses."

"In other words, you're fishing for information," Paula said as she sipped her coffee. "I don't know why you're here. I certainly don't know anything, so you're wasting your time."

Ashford stepped over the railing and sat down at Paula's table. "*Bull!* I know you, Diana, and Terry visited the police a couple of days ago. I know they told you everything. Come on Babe. Work with me. Clue me in on what's happening."

"Ask Terry and Diana to tell you what happened. And don't call me *Babe*."

72

"All right, all right. Look, you know Terry isn't going to tell me anything. Besides, you were a military police officer. You know what's important. You know what the cops are hiding."

Paula smiled at Ashford. She found his attempt to weasel information out of her amusing. "Okay," she said leaning forward and talking in a faint voice, forcing Ashford to lean closer to her. "Here's what the police don't want the public to know. They have a secret list of the best doughnut places in the county."

Ashford straightened up while Paula giggled. "Come off of it," Ashford said. "Tell me what's going on."

Paula handed Ashford the newspaper. "Here, read it for yourself. Terry put everything into the article he wrote. The worst part is that he's now made himself a target. Maybe you shouldn't get too close to him."

"The Runt wrote an editorial. So what?"

Paula tapped the paper, showing Ashford Terry's name in the byline. "He's made it personal. The person who shot Becky now knows he is suspected of several homicides. They're cold cases, which means he thought he got away with it. But now, someone, namely Becky, has turned something up. There is a clue, a lead, possibly even a witness that can put this person behind bars. Right now, this minute, that person has two targets. The first is Becky. He shot her and she's in the hospital, so she's safe at the moment. His second target is Terry. He doesn't know what Terry knows, but he knows Terry is after him."

"So, you think Terry is in danger."

Paula took the paper from Ashford. "No. I know he is."

∞∞∞∞∞

He started a subscription to the paper when he learned that young woman was investigating these old murders. She couldn't leave well enough alone. They were over. He hadn't killed anyone in fifteen years. Besides, he never really meant to kill those women. It was their fault. They shouldn't have done what they did. But now he was really angry. Because of that stupid young blond, others were asking questions. And because of her snooping, that damn hooker he beat up so many years ago sent the reporter a package. He managed to get the package. Then there was this article in the paper. This Terry Lambert threatening to expose him, threatening to *avenge* his fellow reporter. Well, he would show that guy, and everyone else, that threatening him was the wrong thing to do.

∞∞∞∞∞∞

Terry made it a point to stop by the hospital before going to work. He walked in and was greeted by Keiko wagging her tail and Paula smiling. It frightened Terry, especially the part with Paula smiling, until he saw Becky turn her head and look at him.

"Becky, you're awake," Terry shouted as he rushed forward.

Paula shushed him. "Patients are trying to sleep."

Terry walked over to Becky's bed and tried to give her a gentle hug. Keiko saw this as an opportunity to get some attention and managed to get in the way, foiling Terry's awkward attempt. "I can't believe they let you bring a dog into the hospital," Terry said pushing Keiko away.

"Aw, I like her," Becky meekly replied. "She makes me feel safe."

Paula took a sip of her coffee, which she brought from Le Rue. "I'm not supposed to bring Keiko in, but the nurses let me."

Keiko calmed down and returned to Paula's side. "How are you feeling?" Terry asked. "Are you hungry? Do you want me to get you some breakfast?" Terry pointed over his shoulder with his thumb. "I can go down to the cafeteria and get you something. What do you want?"

"Switch to decaf," Paula answered. "She's fine. Relax."

"Paula's right," Becky admitted. "They have given me some really good stuff for the pain, so I'm good as long as I don't move around."

"But are you hungry?" Terry demanded.

Becky giggled. "Don't do that. Don't make me laugh. It hurts. But no, I'm not really hungry. I have a killer headache and am thirsty, but not hungry."

"You're dehydrated," Paula stated. "Even though they put fluids in you via the IV, you're still dehydrated. Once you drink some water, and it will have to be quite a bit, your headache will go away."

"Well now that you're awake," said Terry, "you can tell us about this story you were working on."

"What story?" Becky asked.

"The one about The Sunshine Girl," Terry answered. "We think your investigation of what happened to her is the reason you were shot."

"Get real," Becky argued. "It happened more than thirty years ago. The killer is probably dead. Why should anyone care now?"

Paula stood up and stretched. "I've got to go. Need to get Keiko out of here before management shows up. But Terry's right. You found something, something the killer, who isn't dead, doesn't want found. If you don't believe me, just remember where you are."

"I don't know what it could be," Becky meekly cried. "But maybe if I check my computer, I can find out what it is. My computer has all my files on it?"

"So, you are working on a story," Terry said. "The police took your computer and all your files from work when you were shot. But we met your boyfriend, Thomas, who had a flash drive you gave him. We were able to figure out your password and access your files. That's how we knew about the story you were working on."

Becky sighed. She remained quiet.

"Okay, Terry, that's enough for now," Paula said. "Let her rest. The police are working on the files and there's really nothing we can do about the case at this moment." Paula reached out and patted Becky's hand. "We'll come back later. In the meantime, rest."

"Thanks," said Becky as she slowly waved goodbye to Paula, Keiko, and Terry.

∞∞∞∞∞∞

He was disappointed. Once again there were too many people in that girl's room, especially that tall lady with the large dog. He couldn't do anything with her there. Then that short man showed up.

But today had its good points. He overheard the conversation coming from the girl's room. The tall lady with the dog and the short man were leaving. He was about to enter the young woman's room when a doctor and nurse passed him and walked into her room. He wouldn't be able to silence the girl today, but that didn't matter.

"So, you're Terry," he said to himself. "Good. Now I know who my next target is."

CHAPTER FIFTEEN

Hospital rooms are not designed for crowds, and four police detectives, along with Becky's parents, made the room seem much smaller. Being the only woman detective of the group, Marshall, Freedman, and Oha decided to let Gunn do the talking.

"Ms. Watson," Gunn began.

"Please, call me Becky. My mother's here and it gets confusing when you call us both Ms. Watson."

"Of course," Gunn agreed. "Several days ago, you were shot. We have reason to believe it may have something to do with the story you wrote about a homicide that occurred more than thirty years ago, also known as the Sunshine Girl. I know you've been looking into several other cold cases. Can you tell us what you discovered?"

Becky cleared her throat. "To be honest, nothing. I've gone over everything you had in the reports. I checked the reports from Park Hills that you gave me. The only thing I found was each body was dumped at a different location and all of them were along some rural road without any lights. But you already knew that."

"Who knew you were researching these cases?"

"No one," Becky answered. "I really didn't know what I was looking for, so I really didn't talk to anyone."

"You talked to no one," Gunn queried.

"Well, I interviewed several former street walkers to find out what they knew about some of the victims. But they didn't really know anything and I certainly didn't tell them I was looking for a killer. I told them I was doing an article about the victims."

Freedman stepped forward to attract Becky's attention. "Let me ask you something. Do you know a Tawana Williams?"

"The name sounds familiar, but I don't know who she is," Becky answered.

"She was a former prostitute," Freedman added. "Maybe you interviewed her."

"Possibly. But no one I talked to had anything to say about the murders. A few of them knew one of the victims, but none of them knew anything about who killed them."

"Did you talk to anyone about the Sunshine Girl?" Gunn asked.

"Well, I did talk to one person."

"Who's that?"

"Marianne's sister."

∞∞∞∞∞∞

"Come on, Becky is better, so we've got something to celebrate," Diana said to Lynda and John Watson as they entered Murphy's. "I invited several of Becky's coworkers and friends over; but I think you know most of them." Diana let them to a table where Paula with Keiko, Terry, Wanda, Fitch, and Ashford were already drinking.

"How's Becky doing?" Terry asked before any one of the arriving group had time to take off his or her coat.

"Much better," Lynda answered as she sat down.

"Yes, that's right," John added. "Her condition was upgraded from critical to serious, but stable."

"And they moved her," Lynda interjected. "She's now in a room that's much quieter. I'm sure she'll get the rest she needs. And we met a nice young man that she was seeing. He's with her now. We thought it would be best to let them have some alone time."

"I take it you're talking about Thom Garcia," Wanda replied. "I've met him and he's really nice."

John motioned for a waitress to come over before continuing to comment. "If her condition improves, and I'm sure it will, she can go home in a few days."

Wanda turned to Fitch. "If you don't mind, I can take a couple of days off and clean up her place."

"No problem," Fitch replied.

"Sounds good," Paula added. "But I don't think Becky going back to her place is a good idea."

"You certainly don't want her to stay in the hospital," Fitch said rather loudly.

"Of course not," Paula replied. "It's just that the person who shot her knows where she lives. I think it would be better if Becky went home with John and Lynda until she fully recovers. Even better would be if she could visit a relative who lives out of town."

Lynda snickered. "You don't know Becky very well, do you?"

"I hope you won't take this the wrong way," Paula said, "but I think she's too naïve to handle the danger she's in."

"She's not naïve," John replied. "But, when it comes to being stubborn, she can put a Missouri mule to shame."

"In other words, she won't leave," added Lynda.

"Maybe she could stay with someone until the police catch the guy who shot her?" Fitch suggested. "Didn't the police talk to her today? I'm sure they have some kind of lead on who shot her."

"Oh yes, they talked to her," John replied. "But she wasn't able to give them any information as to who shot her other than it was a man in a dark SUV."

"Well, we can't leave her in the hospital," Fitch insisted. "I would offer to have her stay at our home, but I have my daughter and the grandkids coming to visit next week; and they'll be here for two weeks."

"Well, it looks like it's going to have to be me," Wanda said. "All of you live in single apartments, and we can't have Becky sleeping on your couch. We have a guest room, which we can fix up for her. One of my neighbors is a nurse. She works at the swing shift at the VA hospital, so I can ask her to look in on Becky before she goes to work."

"Hey, I have an extra bedroom at my place," Terry interjected.

"But you can't take care of her."

"Why not?" Terry demanded.

Wanda leaned over to quietly explained, "She's a woman who is going to need assistance with getting to the toilet and bathing."

"You've got a point."

"Besides, we're friends. It will be like a slumber party."

"Oh, that's so kind of you," Lynda said reaching over and patting Wanda's hand. "But it's such a terrible imposition. We couldn't ask that of you."

Paula chuckled. "You're right. It is an imposition. And I hate to put it all on Wanda. But here are your choices. *A*, have Becky go home with her parents and keep her there until we can find the person who shot her. *B*, Becky goes back to her place, and we place an armed guard there, and another one to act as her bodyguard until we catch the shooter. *C*, we let Wanda take her home until it's safe. And for the record, you have only those three choices. So, what will it be?"

"But it's such an imposition," Lynda pleaded.

"Nonsense," Wanda declared. "Happy to do it."

Diana leaned over and placed her hand on Lynda's. "Hey, it's not like Wanda is the only one taking care of Becky. We'll all be helping out."

"Also," Paula added," now that the police know there is a shooter out there, they're going to be looking for him."

"Oh, I don't know," Lynda said, looking at her husband, silently pleading for some guidance.

"Well, I do," Fitch emphatically stated. "Wanda take the next few days off and clean up Becky's apartment."

"I have some time over the next couple of days," Paula said while twirling her drink. "I'll come over and help with the cleaning."

"You don't have to work?" Ashford asked.

"The owner is selling the gym," Paula answered. "Until there is a new owner, I'm out of a job."

Terry waved his glass at Paula. "Why don't you buy the gym? I'm sure the owner would be willing to work something out where you pay a bit at a time. "How long have you worked there?"

"Four years. While the owner is a good guy and would work with me, I still need to come up with a substantial down payment, which is at least fifty thousand dollars, a lot more than I have in my checking account."

"Well, I appreciate the help in cleaning up Becky's place," Wanda responded. "But I can't pay you, and certainly not fifty thousand dollars."

"There's still the problem of getting Becky to agree staying with you," John said pointing to Wanda. "Becky has always been the type of person who would be first in line to help others; but she has a hard time accepting any kind of assistance from anyone for anything."

"She's going to have to learn," Paula replied. "If not, she could end up in worse condition she's in now. She could end up dead."

∞∞∞∞∞

The man couldn't believe his luck. At first, he was happy, even a bit excited, at not seeing anyone visiting the young woman in ICU. The nurses were busy. The staff had gotten so used to seeing him, they started saying good morning and having brief conversations with him. Because of him wearing the scrubs, the nurses assumed he was a doctor. One nurse even offered him coffee and cookies. He made it a point to be friendly, but he didn't like it that the staff was beginning to recognize him. He worked his way to the young woman's room. He was ready to strike. He snuck into the room. Then his anger boiled. The woman was gone. Had she been discharged? He took several deep breaths. Maybe he got lucky, and she died of her wounds. He wouldn't have to do anything. But he had to find out for sure what happened to her.

He exited the room and slowly made his way to the nurses' station. He smiled at the nurse behind the computer. "I see one of your patients have gone," he said, hoping to sound casual as he pointed to the room where the blond had been. I hope she's all right. Did she get to go home?"

Nurse smiled. "No, her condition improved, so she was released from the ICU. She's been transferred to another room."

"Really," he said trying not to sound too interested. "Where did they take her?"

The nurse looked up at him and smiled again. "To the fifth floor. Sorry but I don't know the room number, but the nurses up there do."

"Of course, of course," he said. *Damn it*, he thought, *that damn kid is really becoming hard to kill.*

CHAPTER SIXTEEN
[day seven]

Paula groaned. She was beginning to question why she brought Keiko. The dog was into everything. Wanda brought the key to Becky's apartment and enthusiasm. Paula had the foresight to bring trash bags and cleaning supplies. Meanwhile, Keiko was having too much fun exploring every nook and cranny of the apartment. For Keiko, everything was a game. Wanda filled up a trash bag and started dragging it out. Keiko took this as a signal for a tug of war and she immediately bit into the bag and started dragging it, and Wanda, back into the apartment, managing to spill much of the contents along the way.

"Paula," Wanda yelled. Paula came out of the bedroom where she had been working. Wanda thrust out her hands showing what Keiko had done.

"Sorry about that," Paula apologized. "Maybe I should have left her at home."

Wanda sighed, turned to Keiko, and called to her. "You're a sweet girl," Wanda said in a melodic voice to the dog. "Yes, we love you, but you have to stop this. You're making a mess."

Paula giggled. "You call me over to tell me my dog is causing trouble and you give her T-L-C." Paula pulled out Keiko's lease and put it on her.

"Dogs don't understand. We have to train them that it is what they did that we disapprove of, not them." Wanda reached down again and ruffled Keiko's fur. "She's a sweet dog, and you know I'm an animal lover. I don't want her to think that I don't love her."

Paula attached Keiko's lease to pull her away from the garbage. "Between Becky and you, and everyone else I know at the paper, you're all slightly shy of being normal."

Wanda put her hands on her hips. "Honey, being crazy is what makes the world interesting."

Paula pulled Keiko into the bedroom as Wanda got another trash bag. "Thank goodness there isn't anything icky," Wanda said to herself. She pulled the new trash bag over the old one and started picking up the spilled garbage. She stopped and picked up a single sheet of paper.

"Paula," she yelled, "come here."

"What now," Paula demanded as she entered the room.

Wanda thrusted out a piece of paper. "Look! I found a clue."

Paula took the paper from Wanda. It was information about flights to Springfield, Missouri. Paula noticed the dates for the flights were about a month ago. "Why would she go to Missouri?" Paula asked."

"I really don't know," Wanda answered. "I remember Becky told me about a cousin she had. He was in the army, but he got killed in Afghanistan. They were very close, even though they were just cousins. Now, I don't mean there was anything improper going on. Just that they were very good friends. . ."

"Yeah, yeah," Paula interrupted, "What does that have to do with Becky going to Missouri?"

"Well, he trained at Fort Leonard Wood in Missouri. She told me she visited him when he was stationed there."

"But he's not there now. So why go to Missouri?"

∞∞∞∞∞∞

There has to be a clue in these recordings, Terry thought as he went through them for the fourth time. The recordings showed the inside of the store along with the outside gas pumps from twenty minutes before the victims, Marianne Kesler and Theresa Hallman, entered the store till about thirty minutes after they left. The recording of Marianne showed her and one other woman in the store at the same time. While appeared they may have known each other, the other woman remained in the store after Marianne left. In both cases, the victims bought cigarettes and other items and left alone. The recordings showed them walking down the road alone toward the interstate.

"How's it coming?" Diana asked as she pulled up a chair and sat down next to Terry.

"It's not," Terry answered. "I've watched these recordings and got nothing. But I know Becky saw something here that I'm missing."

Before Diana could say anything, Terry's phone rang. "Good afternoon. *City Times.* Copy editing."

"Yeah, yeah, good afternoon."

Terry put his hand over the mouthpiece. "It's Paula." He turned his attention back to the phone conversation. "Hey what's up?"

"Becky went to Missouri about a month ago," Paula stated. "Do you or anyone at the paper know why?"

"It wasn't for a story for the paper. That much I'm sure of. Why?"

"We found something about Becky going to Missouri."

"Not a secret," Terry replied. "Remember Thomas Garcia told us Becky took off for some place recently."

"Yeah, I remember," Paula answered. "But he didn't know why. I'm betting this trip to Missouri is connected to this case she is working on. See if you can't find out what it is."

Terry quickly checked files on his computer. "I think I found it. According to the article we ran about Marianne Kesler, she was from Lebanon, Missouri."

Paula grunted and took a minute before answering. "The Sunshine Girl. That happen some thirty years ago?"

"That's right," Terry said still staring at his computer screen.

"How old is Becky?" Paula asked Wanda. "She's what, about twenty-five

Wanda shrugged her shoulders. "That's about right. Why?"

Paula stared at Wanda. "Thanks, Terry. I'll talk to you tonight. Let's see if we can't get together at Murphy's." Paula ended the phone conversation. She was still staring at Wanda.

"What?" Wanda pleaded.

"We have a problem," Paula answered. "Becky is investigating a murder that occurred years before she was born. And we need to find out why."

CHAPTER SEVENTEEN

It was not unusual for Terry to be one of the last people to leave the office. As the senior copy editor, he had to ensure the news stories were laid in the paper correctly and edit stories to fit in the space allotted for them. Years of experience made him quite good at the job. Bill Fitch was the only person still at the office when Terry left.

Terry appreciated being able to walk to Murphy's, which was a few blocks away. He hurried down the street, weaving around slower pedestrians blocking his path.

Suddenly, Terry felt a hand grip his jacket and pull him into an alley. The arm spun Terry around and shoved him up against a wall. The person held Terry up, forcing Terry to stand on his toes. Terry caught his wind and stared at a man wearing a long dark coat and a scarf covering his face. Terry could tell the assailant was an older man from the gray hair poking out from under a tattered and worn baseball cap.

"What do you want?" Terry, frightened and off balance, asked.

"You wrote that article, didn't you?" a rough voice from behind the scarf demanded. "Did it do any good? Has anyone called?"

"What article," Terry said almost choking.

"The article in the *City Times* about the old murders, the one asking people to call in."

Terry's throat felt very dry, and he started to let out a series of small coughs. "I don't know what you're talking about. I'm an editor. I don't write news stories. I just make sure the grammar is correct and that kind of stuff."

The masked man relaxed his grip and allowed Terry to stand on the ground. Then he backhanded Terry and threw him against the wall. "Tell me who called. What have you learned?"

The assailant still held Terry. The man backhanded Terry, slapping him twice. "Tell me what you know," he demanded. Terry struggled as the assailant pinned Terry against the wall. Terry noticed a couple of people standing at the entrance to the alley. They had their cell phones out and were recording the incident. Terry weakly held up his hand and pointed toward the people with the cell phones. Terry's attacker let Terry go and roared at the crowd, telling them to leave.

It wasn't much, but it was enough. The assailant was torn between the onlookers and the dwarf. Terry grabbed the assailant's hand and pulled down. He remembered what Paula had told him; bite, kick, scream, do anything; in a street fight; there are no rules. Terry put his head down and butted the man. The assailant took a couple of steps back. This put the man in a perfect position. Terry kicked his assailant in the shins, then he kicked him again. Terry grabbed the nearest thing to him, a cardboard pizza box, and swung it at the man. Although the box inflicted little injury, it did knock the assailant to the ground. Terry kept swinging, hitting the individual on the ground. The man put up his arm to thwart off the attack. Terry dropped the cardboard box and looked around for something else to use as a weapon. This gave the assailant time to stand up. Terry picked up a garbage can lid and swung wildly. The man easily side-stepped Terry's renewed assault. He shoved Terry back against the wall. He grabbed the garbage lid from Terry and started hitting Terry with it. Terry threw up his hands to defend himself. The man grabbed Terry's hands and threw him to the ground. With Terry on the ground, the man started kicking him. Terry put his hands on the ground to get up. The assailant stomped on Terry's left hand. Terry screamed in pain.

"You getting all this," one of the women with a cell phone recording the incident said to the other.

"Of course," the other woman replied.

A boy, about twelve years old, stared at Terry, then the crowd. "Isn't anyone going to do something," he said. "Someone call the police."

The man took a quick glance at the two ladies and the crowd around the boy. He kicked Terry in the stomach before running away. Terry rolled on the ground. By this time, several others had joined the two ladies. The small crowd stood there, watching Terry to see what he would do next.

The boy went over to Terry and helped him stand up. One of the two woman who had been recording the attack put her phone to her ear. Terry was hoping she was calling the police.

CHAPTER EIGHTEEN

Fitch knew something was happening when he saw a small crowd at the entrance of an alley. The crowd started to disperse by the time Fitch got there. He turned to see a boy helping a person get up off the ground. *Someone got mugged*, Fitch thought, *and these people just stood around and watched. What a bunch of vultures.* The victim stood up. "Crap," yelled Fitch. "Terry, Terry, what happened?"

"Thanks kid," Terry said to the boy he was leaning on. He turned to Fitch. "What are you doing here?"

"Right now, taking care of you. What happened?"

"I was attacked. I was on my way to Murphy's when some guy grabbed me and dragged me into this alley."

"You should have seen it," the boy said. "This guy was getting beat up and everything."

Fitch put his hand on the child. "And you came to his rescue?"

"Nah," the kid answered. "The guy beating him up saw all of us over there. I guess he got spooked and ran off."

Terry stood up on his own. "Thanks to you. There were several people there, but this kid is the only one who came to help."

Fitch reached out and shook the boy's hand. "What's your name, son?"

"Why?"

"Because I want to call you something other than kid," Fitch replied.

"Why do you want to know? Are you a cop?"

Fitch snickered. "I'm too old, too fat, and too tired to be a cop. I'm newsman. I work with Terry, the person you helped. Fitch pulled out one of his business cards. "Write your name and address on the back of this card."

"Why," the boy asked slowly. "What are you going to do with it?"

"You're a witness to a crime. The police will want to ask you some questions. I hope you'll help them out and answer them."

"No man. I don't want to get involved. Besides, all I did was help this guy get up after the other guy ran off."

Terry could tell the boy was anxious about becoming involved in a police investigation. "Don't worry about it. If the police come to talk to you, you just need to tell them what happened. It's no big deal."

The boy took a step back and shook his head. "I don't know. I'm just a kid. Maybe I shouldn't get involved. Look, I've got to be going." The kid nodded goodbye and took off down the street.

"He's a good kid," Terry stated. "Out of all the people standing around, he was the only one who came over to help."

"I agree, he's a good kid," Fitch said, "but now let's get you to the hospital and checked out."

∞∞∞∞∞∞

Terry felt like a fool lying in a bed in the ER. The nurse took his medical history and gave him several ice packs. They took him up to x-ray. A young doctor came in, poked and prodded, and said Terry would be all right, but he needed to get a splint for his hand. While nothing was broken, the doctor said it would be better if he didn't use it for the next few weeks to give the hand a chance to heal. *What a waste,* Terry thought. *I could have done all of this at home. There was no need for me to be here.* To make matters worse, Fitch was there doing his mother hen thing. The guy had the tack of a drunken sailor. But when it came to taking care of his reporters, the man was like a grizzly bear protecting her young. He did get things done.

However, Terry's embarrassment got worse. Fitch called the police. Terry could have handled reporting the incident to a couple of patrol officers. But Fitch made sure Marshall and Freedman came down to take the report.

Marshall stood at Terry's bedside. "The doctor said you're going to be okay. A few lumps and bumps, but nothing really serious."

"Are you sure?" Terry asked. "Maybe you should go and ask his mother. That doctor doesn't seem old enough to tie his shoes."

"It's a sign of old age," Fitch added. "Everyone seems too young to know what they are doing."

"I'm not that old," Terry answered.

"I agree," said Marshall. "So, tell me what happened before you have to collect Medicare."

Terry glared at Marshall. "One more crack like that and I'll smack you with my walker and run you over with my wheelchair."

"I'm terrified. Now, tell me what happened."

"I was walking down the street when this guy grabbed me and started beating the crap out of me."

"That's it?" Freedman said with surprise in his voice. "Some nut case just reaches out and grabs you? For no reason?"

Marshall held up his hand to quiet Freedman. "Did you get a look at this guy?"

"Not really," Terry answered. "He was wearing a long dark coat, had a ball cap covering his hair, and had his face covered with a scarf."

"So, you have no idea who this guy was?" Marshall said to confirm Terry's statement. "You can't give me any kind of description."

"I can tell you he was an older guy," Terry responded. "I saw some gray hair sticking out from his cap. He was medium height and build, but he was strong."

"Did he say anything to you?" Freedman asked.

"No, not really. He did ask if anyone had called. I think he was asking about the stories we ran about Becky being shot and that cold cases she was working on."

"I'm sure of it," Fitch added. "Whoever did this was waiting for Terry. Terry got lucky because the attack attracted a crowd."

Marshall nodded that he understood. "Tell you what. Rest easy tonight. Tomorrow, you can come down to the station and give us a more detailed report. I'm sure whoever jumped you is long gone, so there is no reason to put out a BOLO (be on the lookout) for him. Also, start looking over your shoulder. If someone is after you, he's not going to stop, especially if this attack is connected to Ms. Watson's attack and the Kesler homicide."

A nurse came into the examination area. "Mr. Lambert. Everything is okay. The doctor prescribed some painkillers for you, but I must warn you they will make you drowsy when you use them, so don't drive when you take them. Other than that, you are free to go."

"Thank you," Terry said, struggling to get out of the bed. He got his feet on the floor and waved everyone away.

"Come on," Fitch said. "I'll get a taxi to take you home."

"No, that's okay," Terry replied. "I have something I need to do before going home."

"What's that?" Marshall asked.

"Something personal," was the answer Terry gave him.

CHAPTER NINETEEN

Terry knew he should have gone home. But he was already at the hospital. He had nothing to lose by going up to see Becky. He got off the elevator and walked past the nurse's station to Becky's room. The door was closed. He knocked softly, afraid to disturb the other patients, but determined to see Becky. He listened. There was no answer.

"Can I help you?" a nurse walking up to him asked. "Oh, my goodness, what happened to you?"

"It's a long story, but I'm okay," Terry answered. "I was hoping to see Becky Watson if it's not too late."

"Well visiting hours end in about fifteen minutes. Let me check to see if she's up to any more visitors. She's had quite a few today. Can I have your name?"

"Certainly, it's Terry Lambert. I work with her."

The nurse smiled before going into Becky's room. She returned a minute later. "Ms. Watson will see you now. Don't take too long. Like I said, visiting hours are over soon."

Terry nodded in agreement and entered Becky's room.

"Terry, what happened to you?" Becky demanded.

"I'm okay," Terry said. "Earlier, some guy jumped me, hence the new look complete with bruises. But don't worry. I managed to bruise his knuckles when he hit my face."

"Not exactly an accomplishment. Why did he attack you?"

"He wanted to know if anyone called about the stories we ran about your attack."

Becky gave Terry a confused look. "What stories?"

"I guess you wouldn't know. When you were shot, the paper ran a story about it and offered a reward for anyone with information leading to the arrest of the shooter. A couple of days ago, we discovered you were investigating a cold case, in fact, several cold cases. Well, I wrote an editorial asking for anyone who knew anything to call the police. Tonight, when I got jumped, the person who jumped me wanted to know if anyone called about them."

"Terry, I'm so sorry to hear that. I never wanted anyone to get hurt because of some research I was doing."

"I understand," Terry replied. "What is your connection to these cold cases? What's with your interest in the Sunshine Girl? That happened before you were born."

Becky looked down at her hands and fiddled with her fingers before taking a deep breath. She looked back at Terry. "A couple of months ago, we ran a story about the *Sunshine Girl*. The girl's name was Marianne Kesler. After we ran the story, I found out Marianne's sister is still living."

"You went to visit her."

"Yes," Becky admitted. "I went to Missouri after we ran the story. She lives there, close to her daughter and grandchildren. This woman had been living with the hope her sister was alive. I'm sure she knew in her heart that Marianne was dead, or else she would have contacted her. She even filed a missing person's report with the local authorities. When she found out Marianne was murdered, she was heartbroken."

"But what could you do? The murder occurred more than thirty years ago."

"I was hoping I could bring her some peace, some kind of closure."

"How?"

Becky continued to fiddle with her fingers and the bed sheet. "I started looking into other cold cases."

"Did you find anything?" Terry asked.

"Not sure," Becky answered. "Maybe, but I can't be sure. There seemed to be some cases with similarities, but I need to recheck my research."

Terry sighed. "Then we need to get you out of here."

∞∞∞∞∞∞

Where the hell is he? Paula wondered as she signaled to the waitress to bring her another drink. Keiko raised her head in the hopes of getting a treat.

"What do you want?" Paula asked the dog. She bent down and scratched Keiko under the chin. "Yeah, you're a good dog." Keiko wagged her tail in response to the compliment.

The waitress brought over Paula's drink and took the empty glass. Keiko stared at Paula.

"What? So, I'm having a drink while waiting. What's the big deal?" Keiko continued to stare.

Paula picked up her drink and brought it to her lips. She looked down at the dog. She put the glass down. "Not you too. Don't give me that look."

Keiko turned her head.

"You know what I'm talking about. You're working with that VA counselor who thinks I drink too much. She gives me that same look."

Paula looked at her watch. Terry was more than an hour late. She pulled out her cell phone and called Terry's number. It went to voice mail. She left a message saying she was going home before putting her phone away.

Keiko whined. "Okay," Paula replied. "He's late and I can't reach him, so we can go home. But I'm finishing my drink before we go."

Keiko started wagging her tail.

∞∞∞∞∞∞

Terry exited the hospital. He pulled out his phone and noticed he had a voice mail. He played it. It was from Paula telling him she was leaving Murphy's. He took a deep breath before looking up a taxi's phone number in his contact list.

"Heard about you getting jumped," a woman said.

Terry turned around and saw Detective Gunn.

"Glad to see you're okay," she said.

Terry held up his hand. "Not quite. I mean I'll live; he definitely got the better of me. What are you doing here?"

"Came down to see you. Nick called me. He thinks you and Ms. Watson may be onto something related to the cold cases I'm working."

"Nick? Who's Nick?"

"Detective Marshall," Gunn answered.

"Sorry. I forgot his first name. So, what can I do for you Detective Gunn?"

"Let's start with you calling me Jennifer," she replied.

"Sure thing. So, what can I do for you Jennifer?"

"Tell me what happened."

"I already gave my statement to Detective Marshall."

"I know. But if you don't mind Mr. Lambert. . ."

"Terry. If I'm calling you Jennifer, then you're calling me Terry."

The woman detective smiled. "Okay Terry. Tell you what. Let me buy you a cup of coffee and you can tell me what happened."

Terry looked at his watch. "Would you mind changing that to a beer?"

"Not at all," Jennifer replied. She put her arm around Terry's and led him away.

∞∞∞∞∞∞

"We have breaking news," the TV news announcer said. "This is just in. Only a few hours ago, a man was brutally attacked downtown. With complete details, here is Melony Hernandez." An attractive young woman with short brown hair appeared on the screen. She was standing on the street at the entrance to the alley. "Yes, here, just a few short hours ago, a man was walking down Broad Street when he was dragged into the alley behind me and beaten. The cause is not known at this time and the police are investigating. We have dramatic video of what happened."

The TV screen displayed a cell phone video of Terry being beaten. It showed Terry being held against a wall, then Terry kicking the assailant before grabbing a cardboard box and striking the assailant. It showed Terry dropping the box, looking around, and grabbing a trash can lid. The video continued with the assailant getting up and striking

Terry several times before turning and running away. It ended with a kid running up to help Terry. The next scene showed the woman who had recorded it. The woman's name, Vanessa Brown, appeared in subtitles as she spoke. "I was walking home from work with my friend, Beth, when we heard these sounds coming from the alley. We looked and saw this large man hitting this much smaller guy. The little guy tried to fight back, but the bigger one just beat the crap out of him."

Melony reappeared on the screen. The camera zoomed in down the alley. "We have no information on the victim or his condition. Anyone with any information about this case is asked to contact the police at. . ."

"Crap," Terry said to himself. He had been in a good mood after talking to Jennifer. She listened while he explained what had happened. Then they chatted a while before calling it a night. It wasn't a date, but a pleasant exchange. But now his mood had changed. He didn't want to be on the eleven o'clock news. This TV broadcast let everyone know he was attacked. Well, at least he wouldn't have to explain the bruises or the brace on his hand. Still, he wasn't happy about what would happen tomorrow. He would be in the headlines instead of writing them.

∞∞∞∞∞∞

Damn it, he thought as he watched the newscast. *One of those stupid women with the cell phone recorded the attack and sold it to the news station. I guess I should be happy one of them didn't call the police, the dumb bitches. And what is with that damn kid? Who is he? This is getting difficult. And it was all because of that stupid blond reporter. I'm going to have to hurry up and kill her, and the sooner the better.*

CHAPTER TWENTY
[day eight]

Paula stopped kicking the punching bag when Terry walked into the gym a little after six in the morning. She silently reminded herself she needed to lock the door since the gym was officially closed for the week.

"What happened to you?" Paula demanded.

"You didn't hear. I was attacked last night."

"Well, that explains why you didn't show up at Murphy's. But who would want to attack you?"

"I honestly don't know," Terry answered. "I was walking to Murphy's when this guy grabbed me and started beating on me. I think it might have something to do with the cold cases Becky was working on."

Paula held up her hand and started pacing around the room. "Let me get this straight. You were walking to Murphy's and this guy grabbed you. Why do you think this attack is connected to what Becky was working on?"

"He said something. He asked if I was the one who wrote the articles about the cold cases."

"Okay, so he's targeting you. What happened last night? How did you get away?"

"The guy grabbed me and threw me against a wall. At first, he choked me. Then he relaxed his grip, and I started fighting back. I actually knocked him to the ground."

"Then what?" Paula queried.

"Well, I started hitting him with a cardboard box. It wasn't doing much good, so I looked around for something else. He got up and started hitting me. Then he threw me to the ground. When I was on the ground, he smashed my hand."

"I take it you've been to see a doctor."

Terry held up his hand. "Yep, went to the ER last night. They x-rayed it. Nothing broken, but it's going to be sore for quite a while."

"Why are you here?" Paula demanded.

"I want you to show me how to defend myself."

"I already did that. But you screwed it up."

Terry looked confused. "What do you mean? I did what you taught me."

"No, you didn't."

"Yes, I did."

"You didn't run away."

"I couldn't run away," Terry yelled. "He grabbed me. I was walking down the street and I was attacked,"

Paula crossed her arms. "That's not what I'm talking about. You had your attacker on the ground, and you continued the attack. You had the chance to escape, but you stayed and decided to attack your opponent."

Terry shook his head and hands. "I don't understand. What was I supposed to do?"

Paula dropped her arms, leaned forward, and shouted, "Run away."

"Then he would have gotten up and chased me down."

"Not if you ran somewhere public. There would have been witnesses, and maybe someone would have helped you."

Terry shook his head again. "There were witnesses. In fact, one of them recorded the attack and gave it to a TV station. And get this, no one helped me. No one tried to stop this guy."

Paula took a deep breath. "The goal of self-defense in the streets is to escape danger. You use the techniques I taught you to escape."

"But you wouldn't. You would never run away."

"Yes, but I'm a vengeful person and a combat vet."

"And I'm a dwarf."

"Terry, that's not what I meant. I was trained to fight. I'm mean, nasty, unpleasant, whatever."

"That's what I want you to teach me."

Paula reached out and put her hands on Terry's arms. "How can I put this? You're not me. You don't have what it takes to fight like I do."

"Why? Because I'm not a war hero. I don't have any medals for heroism. You think I'm a coward."

"A coward!" Paula shouted. "Are you kidding? Terry one thing you are *not* is a coward." Paula rubbed her hands up and down Terry's arms. "Do you remember the first time we met? It was because of that serial killer."

"Yeah, I remember. You caught the killer."

"What I remember is when he was holding Diana, and she was in danger, it was you who risked your life to save her. That is not the act of a coward."

"But you who caught the bad guy and saved the day."

"Terry, I don't want you to get hurt."

"So, teach me to beat the crap out of people."

"No, I mean yes, I'll teach you; but I've already shown you how to defend yourself."

"What's the problem?" Terry asked.

Paula took a deep breath. "Between you and Becky, you're both driving me crazy."

"What are you talking about?"

Paula turned around and started pacing. She stopped and turned to face Terry. "What if you get hurt? Look what happened to you yesterday. You were beaten because you stayed to fight the guy instead of running away."

"What?" Terry shouted. "You want me to run away?"

"You're not listening."

"What? What?"

"I don't want you to get hurt," Paula yelled. "First, it's that I-love-everybody-waitress-turned-reporter who manages to get herself shot. Then it's you who get beaten by some stranger in an alley. And the two of you expect me to take care of you. You expect me to somehow protect you, to keep you from getting hurt, to keep you safe. I did that in the

Marine Corps. I had to take Marines into the field, into battle, and bring them back. I can't handle that kind of responsibility anymore."

Terry went over to Paula and took her hands. "We aren't asking you to keep us safe. We know you can't protect us from harm, especially when we get into danger. What we need is to learn to take care of ourselves. You did a great job is showing us how before."

"Well, I haven't done a very good job of that, have I? Look at Becky. She's in the hospital. And you. You got beat up."

"Hey, you didn't do this. Someone else did it. You haven't failed us. The world is full of bad guys. We're asking you to show us how to take care of ourselves when we come up against them."

Paula pulled her hands away from Terry's and crossed her arms. She took several deep breaths, trying to think of how to answer Terry. She turned, walked over, and picked up a water bottle. She took a drink and pointed the water bottle at Terry. "Well, with your hand like that, you're limited in what you can do. Still, I could show you a few tricks. But remember the goal here is to escape from the attacker, not beat him up."

"Fine," Terry answered with a huff, "as long as you teach me how to hurt the bastard who did this to me."

Paula chuckled. "Come on. Let's turn you into a warrior."

∞∞∞∞∞

"You know, I love it when you bring your therapy dog with you to our sessions," Cathy Jeffers said as she sat down behind her desk. She brought up Paula's file on her computer screen.

"Keiko's not a therapy dog," Paula replied. "I have a lot of errands to do, and I hate to leave her alone in the apartment."

"Well, she's a sweetheart," Cathy said to the dog. "So, tell me. How are things today?"

"The same as last time."

"You're not going to walk out on our session, are you?"

Paula took a deep breath. "I'll try not to."

Cathy clasped her hands together and stared at Paula. "Look, I honestly understand what you are going through. It's my job to help veterans readjust after serving, regardless of how long they have been out. But I can't help you if you are going to be defensive about everything I say or do. Now, if you want to see a different counselor, that's okay. If not, then cut the crap and work with me. What's going on in your life? Last time you were here, you told me a friend of yours was in the hospital. How is she doing?"

"Actually, she's doing much better. She's out of the ICU and should be released from the hospital in a couple of days. But another friend got beaten up yesterday."

"Oh, my goodness. Was he hurt?"

"Mostly lumps and bumps. His hand is messed up, but he will be okay in a week or two."

"That's good," Cathy gleefully said. "What about your job? You said something about the owner selling the gym where you work."

"That's still happening."

"Any news on who's buying it?"

"So far, no one is that I know of."

"Have you considered buying it? You could get a VA loan. If you take it over without having to close the place, you won't lose any clients."

"I couldn't afford it."

"Why not? You're well paid. I'm assuming the place is making money."

"Yeah. It's doing well. But owning it. I mean there's employee schedules, paying bills, taxes, insurance, etc."

Cathy leaned back in her chair. "When you were in the Marine Corps, you worked as an investigator, am I correct?"

"So?"

"At a crime scene, there is crowd control, evidence collection, taking statements, dealing with witnesses and suspects, etc."

"Again, so?"

"If you were able to handle all of that responsibility, along with taking care of the Marines under you, why can't you handle the responsibility of taking care of a business?"

Paula glared at Cathy. The VA counselor glared back. "You're not walking out this time," she said. "We're going to talk about this, not matter how pissed off you get."

Paula threw her head back and sighed. It was going to be a long fifty minutes.

∞∞∞∞∞∞

Terry got to work at nine o'clock. His hand caused him some discomfort, and he had to stop several times to rest it. He found placing warm towels, which he heated in the office microwave, provided some comfort.

It was after lunch when Fitch approached Terry and handed him a piece of paper. "Here's an editorial I want to run in tomorrow's edition. Let me know if there's a problem." Fitch returned to his office

Terry read the paper. He got up and went into Fitch's office. He placed it on Fitch's desk, sighed deeply. "Do you think this is a good idea? I really don't want to become the center of attention for a news story."

"The story is not about you," Fitch replied. "It's about what happened to you. More importantly, it might give us a lead on who shot Becky. Do you know why I gave it to you?"

"No," Terry answered.

"Because it affects you. People will talk. You'll get phone calls asking for a statement. It could even force whoever attacked you the first time to come after you again. If this bothers you, then don't run it."

"If I don't run it, it kind of makes me a coward, doesn't it?"

"No, it doesn't," Fitch answered. "You know what will happen. Just because you don't want to deal with it, doesn't make you a coward. Some people might even call it a smart decision."

Terry picked up the paper, took a deep breath and let out a sigh. "Okay. I'll lay it in. But will the paper back me up if there are any issues?"

Fitch put his hand on Terry's shoulder. "Both the paper and I will back you. And I'm sure several others here will give you their support as well. Oh, leave out the part about that kid helping. I don't want to place him in any kind of danger from other reporters, or the assailant."

Terry smiled and started typing.

> *The other day, a reporter from this newspaper was brutally attacked. He was walking down the street when a man grabbed him and began to beat him. Several citizens gathered and watched. None of them did anything to help. Once the assailant realized there were witnesses, he ran off. But what did our upstanding citizens do? Nothing. No one called the police or an ambulance. They simply went home. However, two of them recorded the attack on their cell phones. But they did not make these recordings to turn over as evidence to the police. No, they made the recordings to sell to a local news station. They were more interested in getting their fifteen minutes of fame than they were of helping a victim of a vicious attack.*
>
> *What does this say about our society when we are more motivated to get our names in the media than we are doing something to help others, especially when those people are in need? We live in a digital age where we are more concerned about the number of likes on our Facebook posts and the number of X followers than caring about others. People complain about how our society ignores the problems it faces. That's not true. It seems people will notice social problems if it gets their names in the news.*

Terry was smiling as he finished the editorial. The press was fighting back. Maybe they would find this killer after all.

CHAPTER TWENTY-ONE

It was late afternoon and the building shadows shielded Paula from the sun. *I hate that VA counselor* Paula thought as she waited with Keiko outside the City Times Building. *The worst thing is she's right. Why am I afraid to accept the responsibility of running a business? I can do it. Too bad I don't have the money for a down payment.* Paula remembered what she heard so often in the Marines, *"Woulda, coulda, shoulda, s#$%. If you're going to do it, you will solve the problems. If not, just admit it to yourself that you don't want to try."*

Keiko barked. Terry turned to see Paula and Keiko. "What are you doing here?"

"Keiko is here to make sure no one bothers you as you go to Murphy's. I'm along to keep her out of trouble."

"First of all," Terry said with his hands on his hips, "who said I was going to Murphy's?"

"I did," Paula answered. "I called a meeting of everyone involved. I told them to meet us at Murphy's. Your being attacked last night, as well as Becky being shot, means somebody has discovered something that leads to the killer. I thought it might be a good idea to review what we know and plan our next move."

"Why didn't you call me?" Terry asked.

"Because you would have thought it was a pity party and not come. I need you there, so, Keiko is escorting you to a bar where you will bare your soul and we'll get drunk."

Terry stood there for a few seconds trying to think of a response. "What if I don't want to get drunk?"

"That's your decision. But whatever you do, don't try to stop me," Paula replied as she tugged on Keiko's lease. The three of them walked the few blocks to Murphy's in silence. For Terry, it was a relief. For Paula, it was normal. For Keiko, it was a warning that something wasn't right.

Keiko barked.

Paula turned to see what attracted the dog's attention. She saw an elderly man holding a boy who was trying to get away.

"Hey. That's the kid who helped me last night," Terry shouted.

Paula released Keiko's leash. "Keiko! Get him!"

The man glanced over his shoulder just long enough to see a tall blond and a dog running toward him. He pushed the kid away and jumped in a dark SUV and sped off. Keiko ran after the car for a brief time until Paula called her back.

Terry ran up to the kid who was getting up from the sidewalk. "Are you alright?"

The boy looked at him. "Yeah. I'm okay. No big deal."

"No big deal," Paula responded as she picked up Keiko's leash. "Some guy just tried to kidnap you. Why? What does he want with you?"

"I don't know. Probably some creep who likes kids."

Terry shook his head. "No, that's not it. You're the one who helped me last night. I'll bet he wanted to talk to you to see what I said to you."

"Man, all I did was help you get up. I didn't do anything. Hey, I don't want to get involved. Just leave me alone."

"No can do," Terry answered. "I'm pretty sure that's the same guy who attacked me yesterday."

"So what?"

Terry turned to Paula. "Didn't you say that one of the neighbors at Becky's apartment buildings told you the person that shot Becky was driving a dark SUV?"

"Yeah, I did."

"Didn't you also say that person describe the taillights looking like parenthesis?"

Paula took a breath. "And the car that just pulled away had that kind of taillights."

The boy looked at Terry and Paula. "It sounds like you guys are into something that I don't want any part of. Hey, I'm outta here."

"Hold up," Terry said as he pulled one of his business cards out of his wallet. "What's your name?"

Man, I told you. I don't want to get involved."

"Too late. You are involved," Paula retorted. "That guy who tried to pull you into his car. He's not going to give up. He was probably waiting for Terry here when he saw you. That means when he sees you again, and he will, he'll try to grab you. And next time, we won't be here to stop him. So, why don't you tell us your name?"

The kid took a step back.

"Don't," Paula commanded. "You take off running and I'll have my dog chase you down. And I don't care how fast you think you are; you're not going to outrun my dog. Now tell me your name."

"Randy."

"Randy?"

The kid glared at Paula. "Actually, it's Randal Coffey, but everyone calls me Randy."

"Well, Randy," Paula said to the kid, "you are involved and it's time for you to talk to the police."

"No way," Randy shouted. "Snitches get stitches. And that's if they are lucky."

Terry gave Randy his business card. "Let's back up. I understand your reluctance to talk to the cops, but you are in danger. And I mean real danger. It's possible the person who attacked us is a killer. You really need to go to the cops."

"Man, you are really tripping," said Randy. "Why would he want to kill me? The only thing I did yesterday was help you stand up. For all I know, he could have some kind of beef with you."

"What do you need to prove we're telling you the truth?" Paula asked.

"How about some proof," Randy demanded.

"Well, we can show you some files of the past murder cases," Terry replied.

"Are you crazy," Randy shouted. "You guys can be kidnappers for all I know."

"Right," Paula replied sarcastically. "And we're working with the guy who just tried to abduct you. Get real kid."

Terry nodded. "I have an idea. Why don't you come by the editorial office at the paper tomorrow, and I'll show you the proof? You can bring your parents or anyone else you feel safe with."

Randy took a step back. "I don't know."

"Hey, you have my card," said Terry. "It's your choice. But like Paula said, you are in danger. If you don't believe us, think about what just happened."

Randy looked at Terry's card before turning and walking away. Terry and Paula doubted they would see Randy again.

∞∞∞∞∞∞

They entered Murphy's, and Diana stood up to wave to the entering trio. Terry could tell several people were already at one of the long tables. What surprised him was that three of the participants were Marshall, Freedman, and Ashford. A more pleasant surprise was seeing Jennifer there, along with Detective Oha. Wanda had left the table, but she returned with a waitress in tow.

Before she sat down, Paula ordered whiskey and a bowl of water for Keiko. The waitress turned to Terry who ordered a draft beer. In an act of unexpected benevolence, Ashford told the waitress to put the drinks on his tab. The waitress smiled and nodded. Before the young lady could leave, Paula changed her order to two whiskeys.

Everyone at the table exchanged pleasantries, waiting for the waitress to return with their drinks. Fortunately for the participants, the young lady was able to return quickly.

"So, what's up?" Terry asked, hoping to get this inquiry over as quickly as possible.

"Not you," Ashford joked. No one laughed. "Okay, sorry for that." Ashford turned to Paula. "Hey, babe. Why don't you get us started?"

"Don't call me babe unless you have a strong desire to sip your meals through a straw for six weeks while your jaw is wired shut."

Ashford, embarrassed at being admonished, leaned back in his chair. He leaned forward, placing his arms on the table. "Hey, you called the meeting. So, what do you want to talk about?"

Paula gulped half of her drink. "Detective Marshall, find anything new in the files of the cold cases?"

"Actually, the person handling the cold cases is Detective Gunn," Marshall answered.

Jennifer brought out a folder with several police reports in it. "Detective Oha and I went through the files. All the victims fit the same profile; young, attractive, and lived dangerous lifestyles such as prostitution. They were beaten and strangled. All the victims were dumped at night in ditches along rural roads. They were wrapped in either a poncho or a plastic tarp. None of them had any identification on them. The first victim, *The Sunshine Girl*, was listed as a Jane Doe. All the others were identified through their fingerprints or missing person reports."

Paula picked up the reports and quickly looked through each one. "Photos show the victims were wrapped in a green poncho or a brown plastic tarp."

"That's right," Jennifer acknowledged.

"No, you missed the point," Paula argued. "The killer use something waterproof and not very visible. The ponchos are green, like the ones the military uses. The tarps are brown, not blue. Blue ones are more easily seen. He wasn't hiding the bodies, but he wanted them not to be noticed. Also, he used ponchos or plastic tarps to keep blood from getting into his car. This killer knew what he was doing."

"Yeah, we figured that out too," Oha said. "The theory is the killer was a cop or someone who knew forensics. He knew how to cover his tracks. He took the victims' identification with him every time. Nothing was found at the scene that could identify any of the victims. The killer took most of their personal effects with him and dumped the bodies."

"But what I don't get is what did Becky find?" Wanda asked. "I mean, you cops had all this information and the killer felt safe. What did Becky do that you didn't do?"

"Couldn't tell you," Jennifer answered. "But there is also the attack on Terry, and he hasn't done any kind of research on these cases. It's obvious that you reporters are onto something, and we need to find out what it is."

"I don't think so," Terry replied. "The person who attacked me wanted to know if anyone had called about the articles I had written. If he thought I had access to information about him, he would have just shot me like he did Becky."

Jennifer reached out and patted Terry on his uninjured hand. "You're probably right. Your coworker could have found out something that could lead us to identify the killer. We did find out that she visited the Park Hills Police Department three weeks before she was shot."

"Why Park Hills?" a puzzled Ashford asked.

Paula held up three police reports. "Because of Kathleen Cuprio, Amy Morrow, and Melissa Barlett. They were murdered in Park Hills' jurisdiction, and they all fit the same pattern of our cold cases."

"More cold cases," Diana exclaimed. "It's possible this killer traveled all over the state. He could have even traveled all over the United States."

"You're missing the point," Marshall said. "It's not what he could have done; it's what he has done within the past few weeks. He's killed before. He shot your friend and attacked Terry. Also, there's another development. We have a homicide where the victim was shot with the same weapon as your friend. This killer is active again. He's not going to have any problem killing and currently, you're the targets."

Jennifer turned to Terry. "Especially you and Ms. Watson."

CHAPTER TWENTY-TWO
[day nine]

"I can't believe you talked me into this," Terry said as he stared out the passenger window of Paula's car. "Isn't this kind of kidnapping?"

Paula snickered. "You thought this was a clever idea last night at Murphy's. Besides, your editor gave you time off. What would you do instead? Probably stay home and pout."

"So, why do you care?"

"I don't. I have enough problems of my own."

"That's right. Have you heard anything about the gym?"

"Not yet, but Sam hasn't put it on the market yet. He needs to get the books in order first."

"What about you? How are you going to get by?"

Paula reached over and patted Terry on the arm. "Don't worry about me. I have enough saved up to see me through for a couple of months. Once we get this killer, I'll start looking for another job. Trust me. I'll get by. But since we're talking about what's going on. What's going on with you and that detective?"

"What do you mean?"

"I mean that female detective. She took an active interest in this case and you."

"You mean Jennifer?"

"Oh, it's Jennifer," Paula said in a melodic voice which sounded both menacing and silly at the same time.

"Hey, she's the lead detective on the cold cases."

"You're not a cold case. I think she has the hots for you."

"I think you need to see a psychiatrist."

"Already seeing one at the VA."

∞∞∞∞∞∞

A chime went off as Terry and Paula entered Stranden's Convenience Store. A man in his forties, with a dark complexion and a heavy accent greeted them. "Good morning," he said, "Will you be wanting some gas?"

Paula turned to see which pump her car was parked at. "Sure, give me ten dollars on number four." She handed the store owner a ten-dollar bill. Terry started wandering up and down the aisles, looking at the displays. Paula returned to her car and pumped the gas. When she was finished, she pulled her car into a parking space in front of the store.

The chime rang again as she entered. "Got any Red Bull or energy drinks?" she asked.

"Yes," the owner answered in a heavily accented voice, "in the cooler in back."

Paula went back to the cooler and pulled out two drinks. She returned to the counter to pay for them. "It's three dollars for two of them, right?"

"Plus tax. That makes it three dollar and twenty-four cent." Paula recognized the dropping of the plural form of nouns. Something many foreigners did when they learned English as a second language.

Terry came up to the counter to join Paula. "Here you go," Paula said handing the owner the money. "Mind if I ask you how long have you been here?"

"Eight year," the owner answered. "When I first came to this country, I work here part-time. But the owner, he died, so I buy the store. Why?"

"Just curious." Paula answered. She noticed several other customers in the store.

"Business is better now," the owner continued. "It used to be just this store. Most people came from the trailer park near here and a hippie commune down the road. But the car dealership across the road opened after they make the exit from the interstate to Highway 431 and Bradley

Road. Before that, you have to drive up the highway for about fifteen mile to get to the interstate. Once it opened, there came that tractor place. Next someone buy up the trailer park and put up new houses. They made that hippie place move. Now, there's those new store down the road near where Highway 431 connect to the interstate."

"So, this place has really changed over the years," Paula commented.

"Yes. The new development really help my business."

Paula picked up her drinks. "Thanks for the info. Take care."

"You too," the owner said to Paula and Terry as they left the store.

Once in the car, Terry turned to Paula. "Well, that was a waste of time."

"What did you expect?" Paula asked. "The last case involving this place was decades ago. So, the place has changed. But look at this road."

"What about it?"

"The roadside is flat. The pavement ends and there is gravel for a couple of feet. It's easy for someone to walk along the road and hitchhike. Also, remember the owner back there told us this road wasn't busy before this road connected to Highway 431."

"I'm missing something here," Terry said.

"It means whoever drove down this road before then was coming from or going to the interstate. I know developers have brought in shops and restaurants toward the interstate, but there used to be trailer parks and a commune in this area when the murders occurred."

"And you think the killer lived in one of the trailer parks?"

"It's a possibility," Paula replied. "Whether the killer lived there or not, I'll bet he had some kind of connection to this area."

CHAPTER TWENTY-THREE

"What are we looking for?" Freedman asked as they entered Tawana's apartment.

"Some air freshener," Marshall answered, "or at least an open window."

"Decomp doesn't go away. It's going to take some serious cleaning to get that smell out of here. Still, I don't know what you hope to find here. We went over this place when we first got the call about the Williams case."

"But we didn't know it was related to those cold cases,"

"So, we are looking for evidence that is decades old. Who keeps evidence that long?"

"A blackmailer."

"If she had evidence relating to a murder, I doubt she would keep it here in her apartment," Freedman said. "She would want to hide somewhere safe; some place where only she could get it. Besides, I don't think she was blackmailing anyone."

"Why do you say that?" Marshall asked.

"Look at this place. It's okay, but nothing fancy. We checked her financials; there wasn't anything there. Nothing unusual. No gambling debts or financial losses. So, where's the money? It isn't in anything here."

"What if it was something collectable? You know, something like stamps," Marshall asked.

"Yeah, yeah. I saw *Charade*, too. Love Alfred Hitchcock movies. Again, she would keep it some place where only she could get it."

Marshall held up his hand. "Unless she just started blackmailing the killer?"

Freedman stared at Marshall. "Where are you going with this?"

"Think about it. If she had been blackmailing this guy for years, why kill her now? Like you said, there is no sign of her spending large amounts of cash. But if she just started, maybe the blackmail victim killed her. There were no signs of forced entry when we first came here. It's possible the killer came here to pay the money but murdered her instead. The victim was dead a week before the reporter was shot."

"I get it. But she was street smart," Freedman added. "We checked her phone records, and there were no unusual calls on it. Also, the phone records for the bar where she worked didn't turn up anything out of the ordinary. So that means she probably had a pre-paid phone that couldn't be traced to her."

"And we found only one phone, because we didn't look for a second phone."

Freedman smiled to show agreement. It took them almost twenty minutes before they found the second phone.

∞∞∞∞∞∞

He didn't know why he was here. He was sure this was the same stretch of road where he had dumped the first body. It was all her fault. She shouldn't have done what she did. He should have never picked her up. He knew hitchhikers were unpredictable, but he thought she was different being so young and pretty. He was wrong. He hadn't meant to kill her, but then it was her fault for making him so angry. Yes, this is where he dumped her. Now, years later, that nosy reporter started investigating the case. She couldn't leave things alone. That reporter forced him to relive all those horrible experiences again.

He got in his car and pulled away from the side of the road. He noticed the road was still fairly deserted, hardly anyone drove down here. In fact, he saw only one car on the road. He took a quick look at the driver. She was that tall blond with the dog, the one he saw the first day he was at the ER. He was worried. That blond made him nervous, and he didn't like being nervous.

∞∞∞∞∞∞

Paula pulled over and parked her car along the side of the road.

"Looks pretty deserted," Terry said looking at the road, which was in the same condition it was thirty-four years ago when the killer dumped Marianne Kesler's body in a ditch on this road. There was a narrow gravel area, falling immediately into a three-foot ditch on both sides of the road. On the other side of the ditches was a three-strand, barbed-wire fence with signs sporadically posted notifying motorists they were passing through Marts State Park, and this was a wildlife protected area. The entrance to the park was four miles down the road.

"Yeah, it is," Paula admitted as she stepped out of her car. "Notice there are no lights and how close the trees are to the road. They would provide shadows at night, making it harder to see anything in the ditch."

Terry got out of the car to join Paula. "Are you sure this is where he dumped the body?"

"According to the report, it was about a quarter mile past mile marker sixty-three, which we passed back there. I'm sure the spot is around here."

"So, what does this prove?" Terry asked.

"How far away do you think that gas station and convenience store is from here?" Paula asked while examining the ground.

"Well, it took us about twenty-five minutes to get here, so I would say maybe fifteen miles."

"Exactly," Paula stated. "These two points, where Marianne was last seen alive and where her body was found, are quite far apart. According to the autopsy report, she was dumped here four or five hours after her death."

"I get it," shouted Terry. "Somehow the killer knew where to dump the body."

"Well, that's one point," Paula admitted. "The other is why was the body in the killer's car for so long? I'm thinking the killer took her somewhere, somewhere quite a distance from here. Something happened and he beat her and strangled her. Once he realized she was dead, he had to get rid of the body. But why here? Why drive for such a long distance to dump a body? Why not just dump it along the road closer to where he killed her?"

"Maybe this place was special for him?"

"No," said Paula. "If it were, then he would have dumped more bodies here. No, I think he was seen and if he dumped the body near where he killed her, people would connect him to the murder. No, he knew this place was deserted, and it was far enough from the crime scene that no one would connect him to the victim."

"But he dumped the others in deserted places too."

"I'm betting after Marianne; he started noticing other places that were deserted and good places for body dumps."

"You mean he was looking for places to hide his victims," Terry said with some dismay in his voice.

"Probably," Paula answered. "This guy knew what he was doing."

CHAPTER TWENTY-FOUR

"This is the way to end the day," Terry said as he sipped his ice-cold beer.

Paula silently nodded her agreement as she gulped down the last of her first drink. She appreciated that Murphy's allowed her to bring Keiko into the bar. The dog had spent the day in the apartment, so it liked being out. Keiko turned her head to stare at Terry in the hopes of garnering attention and a treat.

Terry noticed Keiko's stare. "What does your dog want now? Don't tell me she drinks beer."

Paula reached over and petted Keiko. "Don't know. Why don't you give her some and we'll see? I know she's not getting any of my whiskey."

"Isn't that considered animal cruelty?" said Ashford as he approached Paula and Terry. He pulled out a chair and sat down.

Before Terry could say anything, Paula held up her hand. "You two play nice or I'm going to have Keiko here take a bite out of both of you."

"Hey, I just came over here to be friendly," Ashford replied. "Wanted to find out how's the investigation going on who shot Becky."

"Really," Terry said with a degree of disbelief in his voice.

"Yeah, really," Ashford answered. "I care about her too. I'll admit she's a bit too chipper for a reporter; but she's a nice kid and I don't want to see her hurt."

Terry nodded agreement and raised his glass to Ashford.

"So, how is the investigation going?" Ashford asked. "Any idea who shot her, or why?"

"Zip, zilch, nada, zero, not a clue; does that give you an idea," Paula answered.

A waitress came over and took Ashford's order. It was still Happy Hour, so Paula signaled for two more drinks.

When the young lady left, Ashford turned his attention back to Paula and Terry. "No leads, huh? We know it was that story about that Jane Doe cold case the police identified after all these years that got her shot. All we have to do is find the person who committed that murder."

"How did you know that?" Terry asked in a mocking voice.

Ashford scoffed. "I'm an investigative reporter, remember? All I had to do was go through the stories Becky worked on. The only two that weren't puff pieces were that one and a story about a traffic accident. Doesn't take a genius to figure it out. So, how are we going to identify the killer?"

"Excellent question," Paula replied. "But it also brings up something else."

"What?" asked Terry.

Paula placed her arms on the table. "How did the killer know Becky was looking into that cold case? All the paper did was run a story about the police being able to ID the victim using her DNA. How did the killer know who Becky was?"

"Good point," said Ashford. "Our paper doesn't print photographs of our reporters, even on our internet service."

Terry chuckled, which annoyed Ashford. "You never heard of Facebook? Becky is a millennial. They practically live on social media. I'm sure the killer looked her up on Facebook or something, found pictures of her. . ."

"And where to find her." Paula added. "But how did he know she was researching cold cases? Also, what did she uncover that made her a threat to the killer?"

Terry toyed with his mug of beer. "Well, we can ask her; she gets out of the hospital tomorrow."

"Good idea," Ashford exclaimed. "Let's all go home and get a good night's sleep." He reached over to pat Paula's hand.

Keiko looked at Ashford. Somehow, she knew Paula was going to have a guest spend the night with her.

CHAPTER TWENTY-FIVE
[day ten]

The next morning, Terry took two steps out of the elevator into the editorial office before being confronted by two middle-aged women, one of them screaming, "That's him! He's the one! He caused all the trouble!" Confused, Terry stared at the woman in a striped dress that accented the point she needed to go on a diet. A second woman, wearing tight jeans barely containing her amble figure, turned to Fitch while pointing to Terry.

"What are you going to do about it?" demanded the woman in tight jeans.

"Do about what?" Terry cautiously asked.

Fitch pointed to the woman in jeans. "Terry, meet Ms. Vanessa Brown, and this is her friend, Beth Jensen."

Terry timidly nodded his head. "Nice to meet you."

"Don't give me that 'nice to meet you' crap," Brown bellowed. You wrote an article about us in the newspaper and got us all sorts of crap just because we sent a video into the news."

"No, he didn't," interrupted Fitch. "I wrote that article."

"No, you didn't!" spouted Jensen. "We know who wrote the article, and it was him."

Fitch held up his hands. "First, quit yelling. Second, we, Terry and I are the ones who should be angry."

Jensen stared at Fitch. "What!"

Fitch put his hands on his hips and stared back at the two women. "One of my employees was being attacked, what did you do? You recorded the attack, not as evidence for the police, but so you could get on TV. What's worse, neither of you bothered to help Terry, or even call 9-1-1 for assistance. A man was injured, but *you* did not call for medical help or the police. The only thing *you* were interested in was your fifteen minutes of fame. Well, *you* got it."

Brown started shaking her finger at Fitch. "We're going to sue you for defamation of character. We're going to sue you!"

"Please do," said Fitch. "In fact, if you wish, I'll start making calls to the TV stations and arrange for a press conference this afternoon. Of course, you can explain why you didn't call the police when you realized there was a crime going on. I'm sure there is a reasonable explanation for not calling an ambulance when you saw that Terry was injured."

"We didn't want to get involved," Jensen answered holding her head high. "You never know what could happen, especially if the criminal knows who you are."

"Then why did you send the recording to the TV station and go on television?" Fitch sarcastically asked. "It wasn't because you were good citizens. By the way, how much did the TV station pay you for it?"

"That's none of your business," Jensen loudly stated.

"Fitch leaned forward, his hands still on his hips. "You're right. It's none of my business. But protecting my reporters and employees is. Making sure the public knows the facts, and all the facts, about each and every incident that makes the news is. Reporting on the actions of people who are harming our community through their selfish deeds is. All of that is my business; and I'm exceptionally good at my job."

The two women stared at Fitch, then at Terry. They turned and walked to the elevator. Terry could tell, even though the women were silent, they were very uncomfortable waiting for the elevator doors to open. Fortunately for them, it was less than a minute before they were able to make their exit.

Terry turned to Fitch. "Thanks. Appreciate you sticking up for me."

"Nonsense," Fitch answered. "It was the right thing to do. Besides, I hate people who are willing to get their names in the news but aren't willing to help others."

"Bet you hate people who text and drive too," Terry said smiling.

"Of course. To change the subject; what did you find out yesterday?"

"Nothing much. But Ashford, Paula, and I were talking yesterday. Just how did the guy who killed those women years ago know that Becky was investigating these cold cases? And how did he know her and where she lived?"

"Social media," yelled Ashford from his desk.

"Wow, wish I had thought of that," Terry sarcastically replied. He turned to Fitch. "But it doesn't answer the question how did he know Becky was investigating the cold cases."

"Wanda," Fitch bellowed.

Terry tapped Fitch on the arm. "She's not here. She's picking up Becky from the hospital."

"That's right," Fitch said running his hand over his short grey hair. "Ashford, I'll need you to do it."

"Do what?" Ashford asked.

"I want you to go back to when we ran the story about identifying that Jane Doe. Go through every article Becky wrote after that. Make a list. There might be a connection. No matter what the story is, put it on the list."

"Why me?" Ashford complained. "Why not have the Runt do it?"

"I'm not a runt," Terry answered.

"Knock it off," Fitch interjected. "Ashford, quit calling Terry a runt. As for doing the research, it's simple. You're an investigative reporter. You're out there interviewing people and chasing down stories. You're much more likely to notice a connection between one of Becky's stories and what is happening on the streets than Terry, who is an editor." Fitch turned to Terry. "You're a great editor, but you get stories after others have done all the research. The reporters on the street have access to a lot more information and have contacts who they can call. Of course, you can look too and if you find anything, let me know."

∞∞∞∞∞

Paula kept crossing and uncrossing her legs as the loan manager of the bank reviewed her financial documents and credit history. She looked at the clock on the wall. It was only ten o'clock and she wanted a drink. *Am I really turning into an alcoholic,* she thought. *Here it's morning and I want a drink. This isn't good.*

"Well, Ms. Stanford," the loan manager said as he put down the papers in his hand. "First, I want to thank you for your service to our country. I'm also a veteran, although I served only three years in the army and never left stateside. Also, your credit rating and financial situation look good. The question is how much of a down payment can you make? This is a business loan, not a home mortgage, so there is quite a bit of financial risk involved. While you're taking over a business that is already successful, you really don't have any business experience."

"Yes, I do," Paula argued. "I was an investigator for the Marine Corps. That meant I had to supervise others, manage time and equipment, ensure my Marines completed assigned tasks and their training commitments. As for taking care of money, the gym has an accountant who handles that. I've worked with her on occasions. While I intend for her to manage the actual financial part of the business, I know enough to ensure everything is okay. And if needed, I have access to others who can help me with business plans, details, and running the gym. Basically, I'm taking over an operation that is running smoothly. What I have to do is ensure people are doing their jobs; something I did for years in the Marines."

The loan officer leaned back in his chair. "You know one thing I learned when I was in the army was it's attitude that gets the job done. I believe you can take over and make this place profitable. If you can get me a business plan detailing how you intend to run the business after you take over and a deposit of at least ten percent, I'll see to it you get the loan. After all, us veterans have to stick together."

Paula stood up and put out her hand. The loan officer put out his and shook Paula's. Paula smiled as she left the bank. She managed to convince the bank to take a chance on her. Now she needed to raise the money for the downpayment. She still needed a drink, but she decided it should be a cup of coffee. She felt good about that decision.

CHAPTER TWENTY-SIX

Keiko bounded into the room. She was greeted by a brown, short-haired, dog, half her size. With their tails wagging, they ran around the room.

"Oh, she's so excited," Wanda said opening the front door wide to allow Paula to assist Becky into Wanda's home. "Tarzan gets so few visitors, so he loves company. It's wonderful that he and Keiko get along."

"Tarzan? You call your dog Tarzan?" Paula asked as she walked Becky over to the couch.

"Of course," Wanda replied, "Look at him. He goes *ape* whenever anyone comes over."

Wanda's home was a shrine to the sea and turtles. She had a large-screen TV, a couch, two recliners, a large-area rug, and a dog bed with assorted toys. That was the normal part of the house. In the middle of the room was a six-foot coffee table shaped like a turtle. In addition, there were framed pictures of turtles on the walls and stuffed turtle toys in various places in the room. On the couch, there were two pillows decorated with turtles. There was a set of patio doors leading to the backyard.

Outside of the patio doors was a wooden deck with patio furniture. Next to it was a large square enclosure with a dozen turtles in it. The walls were eighteen inches high, just high enough to keep the turtles in and low enough for Wanda to step over the wall. She had two small plastic wading pools with water for the turtles. They were large enough for them to swim and drink from, but small enough that Wanda could lift one end and empty the water. She put in ramps so the turtles could climb in and out of the pools. In the dirt within the enclosure, she had planted some grass and set several small logs.

Paula walked over to inspect Wanda's turtles. "Just how many of these do you have?"

"About a dozen at the moment," Wanda proudly admitted. "Why? Would you like one? They make great pets."

"Great pets! They're basically moving rocks," Paula answered. "Besides, I have Keiko."

"Don't disrespect turtles," Wanda replied with a hint of disappointment. "They do a lot for the environment, and they don't hurt others. Besides, they bring me good luck."

"Sorry," apologized Paula.

"They are actually kind of entertaining," Becky replied. "I know the one I have, even though he's in a glass terrarium, does some interesting things at times. And they are easy to care for."

"Don't they stink?" Paula asked.

"Not if you clean up after them," Wanda answered. "I change the water every day and give them fresh vegetables, berries, and cereal to eat. I clean up the old stuff and their poop. But they're outside, so there really isn't any odor to deal with."

"What about your dog?"

Wanda waved her hand. "Tarzan knows better than to get in there. At first, he was curious, but now he hardly pays them any attention."

"What do you do with them?" Paula asked while watching the turtles. "You just keep them here?"

"Of course not," Wanda answered. "I get them when they are injured, usually from being on the road and a car hits them. Once they get better, I release them in a park. If they can't fend for themselves, I give them to friends."

Paula watched the turtles for a few seconds. It seemed only one or two of them would move at any time, and then for only a few steps. "Still, I think I'll stick with my dog." As if on cue, Keiko came running into the room. Paula pulled out Keiko's leash and attached it to her collar.

Paula turned her attention to Becky. "How about you? Are you doing, okay?"

Tarzan jumped on the couch and lay down next to Becky. Becky leaned over and started snuggling with the dog. "I'm fine. I have painkillers and some great company. Also, Wanda is here to take care of me. Everything is great."

Paula crossed her arms. "Except the person who shot you is still out there."

∞∞∞∞∞

He was angry. He again managed to gain entry to the hospital and locate the young woman's room. He was careful not to attract anyone's attention as he slipped into her room. His target was not there. The hospital had released her. He missed his opportunity to kill the reporter. Now he had to find her. He knew he couldn't sit in front of her apartment waiting for her. There was too great a chance someone might recognize him from when he shot the young woman. But experience had taught him other ways of observing her.

He returned to the woman's neighborhood, but he made sure to park his vehicle at a park several blocks from the woman's apartment. He walked over to the street where she lived. He slowed his pace to ensure he got to her apartment when no one was outside to see him. He bent down to tie his shoe, giving him the opportunity to set up a mini camera under a bush, ensuring it had a clear view of the blond's apartment building. The camera had a remote feed to his computer. As long as no one moved it, he could watch from his home. It was a perfect way to wait for his target.

CHAPTER TWENTY-SEVEN

Becky was asleep on the couch. Paula discovered the recliners were quite comfortable. After the busy morning with the bank and helping Wanda pick up Becky, Paula welcomed the chance to relax. Keiko and Tarzan were on the floor dozing. Wanda unlocked the front door and came in carrying two bags. "Groceries," she shouted as she entered the kitchen. "I got everything we need for lunch."

Becky stirred but went back to sleep. Paula groaned as she left her comfortable perch. The dogs jumped up and ran to the kitchen.

"What did you get?" Paula asked as she entered the kitchen.

"I got a wonderful grilled chicken. I didn't know if you liked coleslaw or not, so I got some potato salad. And of course, some cake." Wanda proudly pulled a large carrot cake from one of the bags. "How is Becky doing?"

"She's asleep."

"Well wake her up," Wanda commanded. "It's time for lunch and that girl's got to eat."

"What if she's not hungry?"

"Then she can have some cake. There is always room for cake."

When Paula was a military police officer, they told her never argue with a drunk or a crazy person. Paula knew Wanda was not drunk; however, her sanity was a different question. Paula relented and went into the living room to wake up Becky. Keiko and Tarzan remained in the kitchen. Their eyes glued to the chicken and the cake.

As Paula reached down to wake Becky, Paula's phone rang. She pulled it out of her pocket and answered the call. "Hey Babe," said the voice at the other end.

"You call me *babe* again, the next time I see you I will cut off body parts and nail them to my wall. I am not your *babe*. Now, what do you want?"

"Don't get testy," Ashford replied.

"Why did you call?" a frustrated Paula asked.

"Terry and I have been researching the stories Becky worked on. We think we may have found something. Why don't you and Becky come over to the paper and we can check things out?"

Becky was awake and sitting up. She raised her arms. Paula bent down, put one arm around Becky's waist, and helped Becky to stand up. "Who's on the phone?" Becky asked.

"Ashford," Paula answered. "He says he's found something in the stories you wrote."

"What?" Becky asked.

Paula spoke into the phone. "What did you find?"

"I need you and Becky to come down here," Ashford answered. "We need to check a few things out."

Paula huffed but nodded in agreement. "Okay. We'll be there in a few minutes."

"Oh no you won't," Wanda shouted. "First, we're going to eat lunch. Then we can all go down to the paper. Whatever they found, it can wait until after lunch."

Paula grinned. "Looks like our ETA will be a little later."

"What?" asked Ashford.

"Our *estimated time of arrival* will be a bit later. Hang in there. We'll be there when we can, but it's going to be at least an hour.

∞∞∞∞∞∞

Everybody was standing and clapping as a surprised and embarrassed Becky stepped off the elevator into the editorial office.

"Isn't this wonderful," squealed Wanda. "Everybody loves you."

Diana pulled up a rolling chair for Becky. The editorial staff soon surrounded her.

Becky smiled weakly. "Thank you, but all I did was get shot."

"You did more than that," Fitch replied. "You gave us all heart attacks. We were really worried about you, especially the first few days. How are you feeling now?"

"Oh, okay, I guess," Becky answered. "There's some pain, but it really isn't that bad. Besides, I have some medication for it."

"Well do you need anything?" Diana asked. "Would you like something to drink?"

"No, thank you," Becky replied.

"Were you able to give the police a description of the person who shot you?" Fitch asked.

Becky shook her head. "I heard someone call my name. I walked up to this black SUV, and then, wham. The driver shot me. I didn't get a look at him. The only thing I could tell the police was the driver was a white guy and older, about sixty or so."

"Yeah, we kind of figure that," said Terry. "The guy who jumped me was white and older. We're thinking it's the same guy who shot you."

"Yeah, I know," Becky acknowledged. "You told me about the guy attacking you when you visited me in the hospital. But what does it have to do with a story I wrote?"

"Not a story," Ashford interjected, "First was the story about Marianne Kesler, a Jane Doe from 1988 who was identified through DNA testing. A great human-interest piece."

"Thank you," said Becky.

"Then I checked your Facebook and social media," Ashford continued. "There were several entries about you going to Missouri to chase down information about the Sunshine Girl. There were also some entries about some of the other cases you were looking into."

"It's probably social media that led the killer to you," Diana said looking at Paula and Fitch. "That's probably how he found out what you were doing?"

"But Becky hasn't written anything about cold cases recently," Terry added. "Why would he be looking for her now?"

"You're asking the wrong person," Paula answered. "The person we need to ask is Becky." Paula placed her hand on Becky's shoulder. "What we need to know is what you were doing before you were shot. Where did you go? Who did you see? What did you do?"

"Nothing special," said Becky. "I went to Missouri to visit Marianne Kesler's sister. I visited Marianne's grave with her sister. After that, I returned here. I guess I was kind of depressed."

"You depressed?" Ashford said with a slight scoff. "Never."

"Yeah, yeah, she's a real mental case; you all are," Paula said to quiet Ashford before turning her attention to Becky. "Think. Focus on what you did outside of your normal routine."

"Well, nothing unusual."

Paula shook her head. "No, think. Did you go anywhere that you would not normally go? Did you make a special trip to do something? Think on something you did only once."

"Well, the Sunday before I was shot, I did visit a convenience store on Bradley Road. It was the same one that Marianne visited before she was killed. I also walked down the road for about a mile. Then I went out to Snyder Road where Marianne's body was discovered and placed some flowers there."

"Good," Paula replied. "Anything else?"

Becky shook her head. "No."

"Really," Paula asked with skepticism. "Nothing out of the ordinary? Nothing unusual?"

"Well," Becky answered drawing out the word. "The weekend before I was shot, I got a strange feeling. I came home and I think someone had been in my apartment."

"Why is that?" Fitch asked.

"It's hard to explain. I got the feeling someone had been there. It seemed some things were moved. I don't mean like being moved from one place in the room to other side. It was more of being moved a few inches, like things were out of place. And, it wasn't just one or two things, but several things. I didn't think much of it because nothing was missing or broken. I mean the lamp was over to the side too much instead of being in the middle of the table, the mail was in the wrong place, or the chair was pulled out instead of being pushed in close to the desk. That kind of stuff."

"Okay," Paula said patting Becky on the shoulder. "It's possible someone was in your apartment. Why is a good question. Were they looking for something? Did they plant any kind of listening device or camera there? Wanda and I went over to your place to clean it up for you, and we didn't find anything like that."

Becky gasped with disbelief. "Why would anyone want to spy on me?"

Paula nodded. "Good question. What have you found out about the cold cases? Any leads?"

"Not that I know of," Becky answered. "But I've only collected information on them so far. I haven't done anything more than talk to the police."

"Well, the police have your computer and your files," Terry interjected. "They didn't find anything on them. Also, we gave them the files you left with your boyfriend."

Becky blushed. "Thomas isn't exactly my boyfriend."

"You were dating him for a while, right?" Diana asked.

Becky continued to blush and smiled. "Well, yes. We were dating, and I did give a flash drive with a copy of my files. But there wasn't anything on it that identified a killer, or a suspect even."

"Was that everything?" Paula asked. "Were there some other files that the police don't have?"

Becky raised her head and looked at Paula. "Now that you mention it, there might be. I got a package with some papers in it a few days before I was shot. They were about an attack on someone years ago and the person who sent it to me thought it might be the person who killed Marianne Kesler, the Sunshine Girl. I looked them over. I was going to take them into the police, but I was shot before I had a chance to."

"We didn't see anything like that when Paula and I cleaned your apartment," Wanda said with her hand on Becky's shoulder. "I mean we wanted to make sure your place was ready for you when you got out of the hospital. While we looked through everything, it was to make sure we didn't toss anything you might want to keep. We didn't see any kind of package with any kind of report about a person being attacked."

"So, we have nothing," Ashford stated with disappointment.

Wanda placed her arm around Becky. "Now leave the poor dear alone. She's been through a lot, and she doesn't need you harassing her because *you* can't figure out what's going on."

"Wanda's right," said Paula. "But we need to answer three questions. First, how are these victims connected? What do they have in common? Second, how did the killer know Becky was investigating these cases? Was it from the articles she wrote or from her social media posts? If so, how did the killer find her? Was it through social media? Even then, why did he see her as a threat? And last, how do we keep her safe until the killer is caught?"

Becky stood up. "Stop it! I don't want any of you to get involved. I don't want anyone else to get hurt because of me and my stupid idea that I could find Marianne's killer. It's not worth it."

The editorial staff silently looked at each other, unsure of how to respond. Fitch came over, leaned forward, and gave Becky a gentle hug. He released her and stepped back. "You were shot. It was not a warning; it was an attempt to kill you. Terry was attacked. We, the people on this paper, have gone too far to back down now. I know you're scared. You would be a fool not to be. But you are not alone. We are here to protect you."

"How?" Becky demanded.

"By not backing down," Paula said. "We don't let the killer scare us off."

"Okay," Becky said sniffling, "what do we do now?"

"We have a party," Wanda answered with a smile.

CHAPTER TWENTY-EIGHT

"To Becky," Fitch yelled to be heard above the crowd at Murphy's. The bar was crowded with patrons enjoying Happy Hour and the two-for-one drinks. Most of the editorial staff were there along with Paula and Keiko, Becky, and her parents, Lynda and John Watson. The group raised their glasses for the toast.

Becky nodded to thank everyone for their support. She leaned over to Paula. "I'm not used to being the center of attention. I really don't know what to do."

"Enjoy the spotlight," Paula answered. "We're here to celebrate your recovery."

"Just because I was released from the hospital doesn't mean I'm recovered. I really shouldn't be out. I should be at home resting."

Wanda put her hand on top of Becky's. "Drink your ginger ale dear. After that, I'll take you back to my place."

"Do you mind if Keiko and I come with you?" Paula asked as she drained her first glass of whiskey. She paused a moment before reaching for her second glass.

"Of course not," Wanda happily agreed. "I would love it. The more the merrier."

"I wasn't thinking of having a party. I just want to make sure Becky's safe."

Wanda gave Paula a wink. "That's why I'm so happy you're coming home with us."

"What about Larry, your husband? Will he mind?"

Wanda chuckled. "He's on a fishing trip. Won't be back for a week."

Ashford gave his glass a slight wave at Paula. "Hey, I'll be glad. . ."

"Don't you dare call me *babe*," Paula said cutting Ashford's comment short. "Besides, with Wanda, Becky, me, and two dogs; I think we're safe. You can go over and protect Becky some other time."

Ashford reached over to touch Paula's hand. "Don't say it," Paula demanded. "Not in the mood."

"I hate to say it," Fitch commented, "but she has a good point."

"What?" Terry asked as he sipped his beer. "Ashford's not getting lucky tonight?"

"No," Fitch replied. "We need to make sure Becky is safe. She can't stay at Wanda's forever. Even then, how can we be sure the killer won't find Becky there? We need to find some way of protecting her until the killer is caught."

"Well, I'm not giving up until the killer is caught," Becky stated. "Besides, he shot me and I'm pissed."

"Oh, my goodness," Lynda exclaimed. "That's it. John. We're taking her home with us. I'm not going to leave her while she's in danger."

"No Mom, you're not. I'm not going to put you in danger I'm safer with Wanda and Paula than I would be with you."

Paula turned to Becky's parents. "While I think Becky should go and visit some out of town relative so that she's out of harm's way, I also agree with her. It's time to catch this guy. Marianne and the others deserve it."

"But he's a killer," Lynda said with anxiety in her voice. "Think of how dangerous it will be when you find him."

Paula smiled at Lynda. "I have a nine-millimeter pistol and a dog with an attitude. I'm not the one in danger."

∞∞∞∞∞∞

Paula had a rough night. She had limited herself to two drinks, hardly enough to put her to sleep. At first, Paula was glad she couldn't sleep. She was spending the night at Wanda's, watching over Becky. Keiko was there to keep her company, although the dog spent most of her time playing with Wanda's dog, Tarzan. It was almost two in the morning when Paula fell into a restless sleep.

The time in Iraq haunted her with nightmares that could only be quieted with medication or alcohol. Tonight was no different. She was with a squad of Marines, scouting a small village, when they were ambushed. They immediately took cover. A rocket-propelled grenade hit a building, wounding several Marines. Paula ran over and pulled one of them from the rubble, she turned the person over and saw Becky's face. Paula jumped up before she was fully awake. She stared at the nine-millimeter pistol in her hand. She was thankful she did not have a target to shoot at.

Paula sat back down in the recliner in Wanda's living room. Keiko came over and started nuzzling her to calm her. Paula noticed Wanda's dog, Tarzan, was in a corner hiding.

CHAPTER TWENTY-NINE
[day eleven]

The voices in the kitchen woke Paula. She saw Keiko and Tarzan outside in the yard playing in the morning sun. Paula sat up in the recliner and stretched. As she put her arms down, Becky was standing next to her with a cup of coffee.

"Morning sleepy head. Wondered when you would wake up?"

Paula took the coffee from Becky. "Just waiting for the coffee. No sense in getting up unless there's some ready."

"Right," Becky slowly replied. "So, what are your plans today?"

"Drink coffee. Eat breakfast. Be lazy. And whatever else comes to mind. Why?"

Becky shuffled around the turtle coffee table and took a seat on the couch, facing Paula. "Yesterday, you asked if I had talked to anyone about the killings. While I didn't talk about the killings, I did interview a few people who knew some of the victims. Most of them were dead ends. They didn't remember the victim, or really didn't know anything, which isn't surprising since these murders took place so long ago. But there was one woman who acted a bit strange."

"How? In what way was she strange?"

"The woman was awfully nervous, like scared. She denied knowing anything, but she kept staring at one of the photos of the victims. I think she knew the woman in the photo."

"Are you sure?"

Becky shrugged her shoulders. "It's more of a hunch. I didn't think much of it at the time. But last night, when you asked about the people

135

I interviewed, I started thinking. This one woman sticks out in my mind."

"Who was she?" Paula asked.

"I don't remember. I'm sure I have her name and info back at my apartment. We can go there later and pick it up."

"Sure," Paula replied. "But first coffee. Then, we take on the world."

∞∞∞∞∞∞

He kept flicking through the selections on Netflix. Even with hundreds of movies and TV programs, nothing interested him. His interest was the video feed on his computer. Every few seconds he would stare at the computer monitor. The camera showed the reporter's apartment building, but so far, the only things he saw were neighbors walking their dogs and the packages being delivered. He got up and went into the kitchen. He opened the refrigerator, looking for something to eat. He wasn't hungry. He was bored. He closed the refrigerator door and went to the cupboard to pull out a bag of potato chips. He returned to his chair in front of the television. Movement on the computer screen caught his attention. He smiled and put away the potato chips.

∞∞∞∞∞∞

Paula parked on the street in front of Becky's apartment. Paula went around to the passenger side to help Becky out of the car.

Paula put out her arm to help Becky, but Becky waved it off. "I'm fine," Becky stated. "I may not be able to dance, but I can certainly walk to my apartment."

Becky pulled out her keys and opened the door to her place. "Welcome to my humble abode. My goodness, you guys really cleaned the place up."

The apartment was modest. The living room furniture was limited to a large, brown easy chair with a matching couch; a small, two-door cabinet supporting a television; and a small stool being used as an end table next to the easy chair. The only light was the one in the ceiling fan. The last piece of furniture in the room was a press-wood desk where her computer had been along with her printer and several books.

"Yeah," Paula responded. "Wanda and I wanted you to come home to clean place. It didn't take much. You weren't that messy. Oh, also the police were here. They took your computer and looked through your notes for clues to who would want to shoot you."

"You mean they took all my notes? You should have said something. We'll never find her name if they took my notes."

Paula groaned as she sat down on the couch. "Don't know what's wrong with me. I should have realized the police would have taken any notes you had. Sorry. Guess this is a wasted trip."

"Maybe not," Becky said as she began to gather a few things in the apartment. "I need to pick up some things to take back to Wanda's if I'm going to stay there. Then we can stop by the police station and see if they are finished with my computer and notes."

"Sounds like a plan," Paula replied. "I'll just hang out while you pack."

∞∞∞∞∞∞

He had to rush. He didn't know how long that blond reporter would be at her apartment. He didn't want to have to deal with any other people.

He picked up the luggage tracker he purchased off the internet. He painted over the numbers on the tracker and taped several strong magnets to it. He had tested it a couple of days before to make sure it would work. His big concern was the car. Nowadays, most cars have less metal, which would make it difficult to attach to the vehicle. But he knew if he could get under the car, he would find a place to put it.

He smiled as he pulled onto the street where the blond girl's apartment was located. He drove past a car. It was the car he had seen the blond woman with the dog driving the day before. He knew it was the car she and the reporter used to get here. He parked about fifty feet away. He slowly got out of his car and took a moment to see if anyone was outside. It would ruin everything if a neighbor was out watering the lawn or walking a dog. The streets were empty. He started walking toward his target. He approached the driver's side of the vehicle. A quick look confirmed nobody was inside the car. He ducked down and felt around the rear wheel well, hoping to find metal located behind it. His quest was successful. He carefully placed the luggage tracker so that it was out of sight and made sure it was secure. He got up and checked to see if anyone was in the area. He returned to his vehicle and pulled away from the curb. Halfway down the street he saw a woman walking her dog. He waved to her as he left the apartment complex.

CHAPTER THIRTY

Terry wasn't comfortable standing in the press briefing room at the police station. He was up front with the flag of the United States on one side and the state flag on the other. In the center was a lectern, which was as tall as he was. Bill Fitch and Detectives Jennifer Gunn and Steven Oha were next to Terry. On the opposite side of the lectern stood Vanessa Brown and Beth Jensen along with a man in a three-piece suit. Seated in four rows of chairs were several reporters, including Ashford Zane. Along the sides of the room were reporters with television cameras.

The man in the suit approached the lectern and cleared his throat. "I'm Edward Tyler, here representing Ms. Brown and Ms. Jensen concerning the outrageous allegations made by *City Times* about how they neglect their civic duty to assist the police with any active investigation.

"They weren't allegations; they were facts," Fitch stated in a firm voice.

Detective Gunn placed her hand on Fitch's sleeve and signaled for him to allow the lawyer to continue.

The lawyer glared at Fitch. "I was saying, today we are here to prove that my clients are willing and happy to cooperate with law enforcement. Several nights ago, Ms. Brown and Ms. Jensen witnessed an assault taking place and they had the presence of mind to record the crime. They are here today to turn over that evidence to the police, in hopes it will help them find the perpetrator and make an arrest."

A reporter raised his hand. Before the lawyer could acknowledge him, the reporter shouted. "Why were the recordings released to a TV's news station earlier? Why wait until now to bring the recordings to the police?"

"I'll tell you why," Fitch responded. "It's because one of our reporters was shot and another member of the paper was assaulted. And we are taking a stand against citizens who refuse to cooperate with the police. These are serious crimes, resulting in two individuals requiring medical attention. And the person who committed these crimes is still out there. *And he's dangerous.* We need people to understand the police cannot do their job unless we, the public, work with them. Crime affects all of us."

"Sir," the lawyer yelled. "Please get off your high horse. My clients are cooperating, and they are doing their civic duty."

Fitch didn't back down and started shouting back. Within seconds the lawyer and Fitch were shouting back and forth while reporters competed for attention with their questions. Soon, Ms. Brown and Ms. Jensen joined the lawyer in yelling at Fitch. Terry took several steps to the side, away from Fitch. That's when Terry noticed Paula and Becky entered the room. Detective Gunn allowed the chaotic situation to continue for two more minutes. Two patrol officers entered the room. Detective Gunn motioned for them to come forward. They managed to make their way to the front of the room and to Detective Gunn. She took a baton from one of the patrol officers and walked up to the lectern. With strength and determination, she banged it on the lectern three times. The crowd quieted down.

"Knock it off," she commanded. She pointed the baton at the lawyer. "Have your clients give me the recordings." She turned to Fitch. "You, save the speeches until you run for office." Detective Gunn slowly turned to the media. "This press conference is over. You may interview individuals outside, but one at a time." She returned her gaze to Fitch and the lawyer. "And you two, play nice." Detective Gunn returned the baton to the patrol officer. The patrol officers ushered the reporters outside to the parking lot where several of them set up TV cameras. Terry made it a point to leave by another exit and avoid the reporters.

∞∞∞∞∞

He was in a good mood by the time he got home. He had planted the tracking device without any problems. He turned on his computer. After a few moments, he was able to open the program that gave him the location of the tracker. It was working perfectly. He opened a map application. He realized the tracker was at the police station. He then turned on his television. He would have to wait to see if the tracker moved. If it didn't move, it meant the tall blond with the dog probably found it and turned it over to the police. He switched the channel to the news to get an idea of the weather for the next few days. Instead, there was a special report about an incident at the police station. What caught his interest was in the background he could see the blond he had shot. She was at the police station. He was no longer in a good mood.

CHAPTER THIRTY-ONE

"You just missed your friend," Jennifer stated as Paula and Becky entered the detective's office. "There was a press conference downstairs. It got a bit out of hand. I think Terry left during all the commotion."

"We saw what happened," Becky replied. "But we actually came here for a different reason."

"You want your stuff back," Jennifer answered.

Paula made a pistol gesture with her right hand. "You got it. We stopped by at Detective Marshall's office, and he sent us up here to you."

"Since your attack is related to our cold cases, he sent your computer and files up to us. We may still need it, so I can't release it back to you. But I can assure you that you will get it back once the investigation is over."

"I don't really need to get it back just yet," Becky replied. "I really just need to look at my notes."

"That brings up an interesting point," Jennifer responded. "In your notes, which we did go over, you listed a Tawana Williams, a former prostitute known as *Sweet Tea*."

"Actually, I interviewed several former prostitutes," Becky replied. "What do you want to know about this one?"

"She was killed about a week before you were shot. We need to know what she told you."

Becky cleared her throat. "May I see my notes? I interviewed so many people I need to review my notes to answer your questions."

"Of course," Jennifer said as she handed Becky a folder.

Becky took a seat and spent several minutes going through the contents of the folder. "I did interview Tawana Williams; but from my notes, it looks like she didn't tell me anything. If she had, I would have certainly put in my notes. But there was another person I interviewed who might know something. She was attacked and almost killed. The woman simply refused to discuss it. She stated she could not say anything. But I got the impression she knew or could identify her attacker."

"Why is that?" Jennifer asked.

"Because she said, 'It's too late to do anything about it now. And it's best that I don't.' At first, I thought maybe the killer was dead. But now, I think she's afraid if she identifies him, he'll come after her."

"That's a valid conclusion," Paula replied. "He came after you, and you don't know who he is." Paula motioned to Jennifer. "This other woman may know who this man is. She has good reason to be afraid. We know for certain he's dangerous."

"That's if it's the same man," Jennifer interjected. "Still, it would be nice if we could interview this other woman."

Becky handed the open folder back to Jennifer. "Her name is Cindy Doss. She was attacked in May 1998."

CHAPTER THIRTY-TWO

Cindy glared at the three women standing on her front porch. She turned away and went back into her home.

The door was open. Paula stepped inside the doorway. "I take it you don't mind if we come in."

"Figured someone would be back to ask more questions," Cindy said over her shoulder. She grabbed a bottle of expensive scotch and poured herself a drink. She turned to face Paula, Becky, and Jennifer. She sat down at the dining-room table and motioned for the others to have a seat. Paula noticed the host didn't offer anyone else a drink. She was proud of herself; she wasn't offended by Cindy's lack of courtesy.

Paula took careful note of the woman and her surroundings, as did Becky and Jennifer. Although in her mid-forties, Cindy still had a sensual figure and good looks. Her chestnut brown hair came down past her shoulders and it complimented the plain blue dress she was wearing. The home was tastefully furnished with several landscape prints on the wall. There were several photos of her with her husband and kids, including one of a girl in a baseball uniform and a baby wearing a sailor outfit. Paula stopped to admire the photos of the children.

"Those are old," Cindy said as she took a sip of the scotch. "I really should get some new ones."

"Why?" Paula stated. "They look cute in these."

"I know," Cindy answered. "But every time their friends come over; all I hear is how embarrassed my children are. Can't blame them. They're both teenagers now."

Jennifer took out her ID and badge. "I'm Detective Jennifer Gunn. I believe you know Ms. Becky Watson. The other woman, the one admiring your family photos, is Ms. Paula Stanford. I realize this may be a sensitive topic, but I would like to ask you a few questions about an assault on you several years ago."

"Yeah, I know," Cindy acknowledged. "I knew someone would be by to talk to me after I read what happened to Sweet Tea and Ms. Watson over there."

"So, you knew Ms. Tawana Williams," Jennifer asked.

"Not that well. I remember her because she also got beat up about a year after I did. I read about it in the papers and visited her. From what she told me; it sounded like the same guy beat her up too."

Jennifer nodded her head. "Like I said, I realize this is a sensitive topic, but could you tell us what happened?"

Cindy took another sip of scotch. "It's not that sensitive. My husband knows what I did before I married him. He was a.. a..."

"Client," Paula interjected.

"I like that word," Cindy said with a smile. "Yes, he was a client. Anyway, he knows what I did. This might sound strange, but you do develop a fondness for certain *clients*. Usually, it's because of the way they treat you. Daniel, that's my husband, even remembered my birthday and gave me flowers. After the attack, I quit the profession and found a job working as a waitress in a coffee shop. Several of my *clients*, as you call them, would come by and try to get me to sleep with them. Daniel found out where I worked. He would come by, but he always was more interested in how I was doing instead of trying to get laid. Of course, with all the men coming around, I got fired. Daniel suggested I try working for a friend of his as a kind of Girl Friday. His friend knew what I was, but he was nice and gave me a job. Daniel and I started dating, and I actually fell in love with the guy. We got married and we're happy. Kind of enjoy being the stereotyped family. At least until Ms. Watson showed up."

"Sorry for that," Becky apologized. "I was just researching a story. I didn't mean to cause you any trouble."

Cindy waved her hand to signal it was no problem.

"I hope our visit won't cause you any problem," Jennifer said. "But could you tell us about the night you were attacked?"

"Fortunately, the kids are at school and won't be back for hours," Cindy replied. She took another sip of her scotch. She put down her glass and took a deep breath. "The night of the attack. Well, it began like so many other nights. I was on the street at my usual spot. Cars would pull up. One of us would go and ask the person if he wanted a date. You know the routine. This night, a man in a dark pickup pulled up to the curb. Before any one of us could say anything, he pointed to me and said he wanted me. I went over, talked to him for a minute or two. We agreed on what's to happen. I got in and we went to a motel about a mile down the road. We used the place a lot, so I knew it pretty well and the people there knew us. We got a room, and I started my routine. I flirted with him a little, you know, to get him in the mood. I started to take off my clothes. When I got down to my panties, I stopped. This was where I made sure he's got the money. I lit a cigarette. This guy went nuts. He started screaming for me to put out the cigarette. Then he started coughing, then sneezing, then burping, and finally farting. This guy was doing all of this at the same time. It was kind of funny, so I started giggling. He pointed to the cigarette, so I put it out. He took out an inhaler, took a couple of puffs, and started to calm down. He caught his breath. Then he started yelling at me, saying I shouldn't laugh at him. He said it was a medical condition. Then he started slapping me. I told him that's it; I'm leaving. He grabbed me and punched me several times. He knocked me to the floor and kicked me. I screamed. He was about to kick me again when someone started banging on the door. The guy outside said he's calling the police. The guy beating me waited for the man outside to leave. Then he grabbed his things and left. But before he left, he told me not to tell anyone what happened. He said he works for the state, and he would know if I told the cops anything, and he would come back. I was still on the floor when the cops arrived and called an ambulance. I spent a week in the hospital."

Jennifer looked up from her notes. "What can you tell us about the man who attacked you?"

"He was strong. He was a white guy. He wasn't a big guy, but he was tall. He wasn't fat, but he wasn't skinny either. I remember seeing a uniform with some kind of badge in the truck. He was older than me, so I guess he's in his sixties now. Other than him having such a reaction to cigarettes, I can't think of anything unusual about him."

"You sure there isn't anything else you can tell us about him?" Paula asked.

Cindy took a sip of her scotch. "Well, he can become really mean in a hurry. If that guy hadn't banged on the hotel door, he would have killed me.

∞∞∞∞∞∞

At first, he thought they had found the luggage tracker he had placed on the tall woman's car. But it left the police station and moved to a residential area. He was cautiously optimistic. *Maybe they hadn't found the tracker. Maybe this is where that young blond is hiding.* He realized he needed to check it out.

It didn't take long for him to find the neighborhood. He slowly drove around, looking for signs of police cars or undercover cops staking out the place. Seeing none, he proceeded to the street where the signal was coming from. He saw the car with the tracker parked in front of a two-story house. He drove past the car and parked in front of a house with a for-sale sign in its overgrown lawn. He made sure he could see both the car and the front of the house in his rear-view mirror.

He started to plot ways to sneak in and kill the blond. This was a neighborhood with homes close together. He knew he wouldn't be able to go through anyone's backyard without alerting neighbors' dogs. This was also the kind of neighborhood where people would notice any service trucks. Then there were the popular security cameras so many people had nowadays. He was lucky the first time he tried to kill the blond. He knew she would exit her apartment building to go to work. But now, he had no idea when she would leave this house. He couldn't wait here for any length of time without being noticed. How he wished he could get her out of that house.

As if answering a prayer, his target appeared. She was with the tall woman he had seen before. There was another woman. He didn't recognize her. Finally, a fourth woman came out. It seemed she was saying goodbye to the other three. He was in luck; he didn't need to get into that house after all. He waited until the three women got into the tall woman's car and drove away. He was about to leave when a sense of dread came over him. *Why were those women visiting that house? Was this another problem like that reporter?*

CHAPTER THIRTY-THREE

"It was nice of you to call," Terry said while looking over the menu at The Fatten Ox, one of the best steak houses in town.

Jennifer smiled. "Figured it would be a good time to go over what we've found so far about the cold cases and your friend. We could exchange information."

Terry snickered. "Well, you're going to be disappointed. We haven't found out anything. Paula and I even drove out to the convenience store the Sunshine Girl visited before she died. Then we went to where her body was found."

"And I take it you discovered nothing."

"Well, not quite. Paula pointed out that the girl had been in the killer's car for several hours. She thinks the killer and the victim was seen together some place quite a distance from here. Paula thinks the killer drove her back to this area to keep people who saw them together from connecting her death with him. Paula thinks it may have a two or three-hour or longer drive from here."

"Good point. We knew she was in the vehicle for a while, but we figured it was because he was looking for a good place to dump it. But your friend's idea has merit."

"So, where do you think she was killed?" Terry asked.

"I think it was locally. There are too many body dumps in this area." Jennifer answered. "But your friend's idea explains why the victim was in the killer's car for several hours."

"Were the other victims keep in a car for a long period of time?"

"There's some evidence of them being seated for a while, but not as long as the first victim."

"So, no clues," Terry responded.

"Not quite. Paula, Becky, and I met with a woman who may have been attacked by the killer. Becky had interviewed her when she was researching the cold cases. This woman used to be a prostitute. One night she was beaten by a man who she picked up. Her injuries were like the Sunshine Girl's, who was beaten before she was strangled."

Terry flipped his menu before putting it down. "I would think a lot of prostitutes suffer from beatings. What makes you think her attack was by the same person?"

"The woman told us she knew Tawana Williams. Williams was a former prostitute who was murdered a couple of weeks ago. Remember, we told you the ballistics report showed the same gun was used to kill her and shoot Becky. According to Becky's notes, she did talk to Tawana Williams. But when I talked to Becky, she told me Ms. Williams didn't remember any of the victims and had nothing to say. Then, when we talked to this other woman, she told us Ms. Williams was also attacked, and she thinks it was the same man who attacked her."

"So, the same person who attacked this woman also shot both Becky and Ms. Williams."

"Exactly," Jennifer acknowledged.

Terry fiddled with the menu.

Jennifer patted Terry's hand. "So, what are you going to order?"

"Probably the prime rib. After all, it is a steak house."

Jennifer picked up her menu. "I think I'll go with the prime rib too."

Terry chuckled. "Great. We managed to figure out what to have for dinner. Now, can we figure out how Becky and this Ms. Williams are connected. Becky interviewed her, but why come after them?"

"Let's focus on the injuries. The Sunshine Girl suffered the same kind of injuries our witness had, and so did Tawana Williams, according to our witness. Both Tawana Williams and your friend, Becky, were shot with the same gun. The thing they all have in common is your friend's interest in these murders from so long ago. Therefore, it's logical to believe the killer of the Sunshine Girl, the others, Ms. William's death, your friend's shooting, and your beating; were all committed by the same person."

"That's a logical assumption, but what proof do you have?"

"None. But it's more than we had before."

Terry smirked. "Great a solid lead about someone nobody knows."

"Not quite," Jennifer replied. "We know that at least two of the victims visited the same convenience store before they were murdered. Also, one of the other victims was last seen at a restaurant a few miles from the area."

"Which means the killer knew the area. He probably drove up and down that road regularly."

"That's right."

Terry started jabbing the table with his finger. "I just remembered something else Paula and I found out. There used to be a couple of trailer parks near that convenience store. Maybe the killer lived there."

"That's a good point," Jennifer acknowledged. "The victims could have been at the trailer parks with someone before they went to the store. But there is the question of how they got there and why didn't they get a ride back?"

"Maybe they lived there?"

Jennifer shook her head. "No, we checked their addresses. None of the victims lived there."

"Maybe they were hitchhiking and that's where they got dropped off."

"Who would give them a ride and leave them in the middle of nowhere?"

"It wasn't the middle of nowhere," Terry stressed. "The trailer parks were fairly large. There were several hundred homes out there. Then there was a hippie commune. And the road is well traveled. And the road does lead to Park Hills, the city where you said there were other victims."

"Which means our killer traveled between Park Hills and Fort Stebbins or lived in one of the trailer parks."

"The problem is the trailer parks are gone," Terry stated. "There's no way to find out who lived there thirty some years ago. And it's impossible to find out who drove between Park Hills and Fort Stebbins during that time. Talk about dead ends."

"No, it's not," Jennifer argued. "We have a better profile idea of our killer. It's not great, but it's a step in the right direction."

"Meanwhile, Becky is in danger."

Jennifer crossed her arms in front of her. "Stop being so negative. We have a profile. It's not a good one, but it's a start. We know our killer is the same person who shot your friend. There are now four detectives working on the case, from two different perspectives. And we've got you and the rest of your coworkers researching these cases."

Terry sighed. "I guess you're right. We are making progress."

"And the best thing," Jennifer continued as she uncrossed her arms and held Terry's hand, "Is I get to have dinner with a very interesting person."

CHAPTER THIRTY-FOUR
[day twelve]

Freedman was sitting at his desk with his feet up and enjoying a cup of coffee when Marshall walked into their office. Without saying a word, Marshall went over and poured himself a cup of coffee before taking his place at his desk.

"Morning Grumpy," Freedman said with a smile on his face.

Marshall glared at him, remaining silent. Freedman put his feet down and leaned forward, placing his coffee and arms on his desk.

"Don't," demanded Marshall, "don't you dare tell me it's a beautiful day in the neighborhood."

Freedman snickered. "It's amazing just how jovial you are in the morning."

"I'm on my first cup of coffee. It's too early to be happy."

"But I've got good news."

Marshall waved his coffee mug at Freedman. "Good news is a long-lost relative I don't know left me millions of dollars in his will, and I can retire."

"Well, it's not that good," Freedman replied. "We got the phone records for the second cell phone we found at Tawana Williams' apartment."

"How many calls did she make?"

"From that phone, not many. One was to her old pimp. Not surprisingly, he's in prison. Another to a private investigator, James Whitman. He specializes in finding missing people, mostly dead-beat dads. There is one other number. I tried calling it but got no answer. The number was disconnected."

Marshall groaned as he got up. "When do you think this James Whitman is going to be in his office so that we can pay him a visit?"

Freedman stood up and gave Marshall a friendly pat on the arm as he sauntered over to the door. "We're in luck. He's agreed to meet us for breakfast."

∞∞∞∞∞∞

"Welcome to Denny's," A short black lady said she made her way from behind the counter to greet Marshall and Freedman. She grabbed two laminated menus and motioned for the detectives to follow her.

Whitman was in his late fifties, with a substantial belly requiring a large Aloha shirt to cover it. He had thinning grey hair, a fair complexion, and a pencil-thin moustache. Marshall immediately spotted Whitman among the half dozen patrons in the restaurant. Whitman was sitting with a clear view of the entrance, with a detective novel in his hand, and a cup of coffee and file folder on the table in front of him. The hostess stopped next to Whitman's table and placed the menus on the table.

"How did you know we were here to see him?" Marshall asked.

The hostess pointed to the badges on his and Freedman's belts. She gave Whitman a nod and left.

"Thanks Shelia," Whitman said as she walked away. He gestured for the two detectives to sit down.

"Is this your office?" Marshall asked.

Whitman grinned. "Used to have one, but I spent so much time running around, I realized it was a wasted expense. I find it easier to meet people at their homes, places of business, or here."

"Works for us. Thanks for seeing us," Freedman said as he sat down.

"My pleasure," Whitman replied with a small wave of his hand. "Happy to help out anytime. Used to be a cop myself."

"Really? Where?" Marshall asked.

Whitman pulled out his wallet from which he extracted a retired police ID card. "New York. Got a little too wild and I ended up with a bullet in the leg. Got a disability retirement. Moved here to get away from the big city. The PI stuff keeps me busy and give me an excuse to hit the bars."

"I heard you specialize in finding people," Freedman stated.

Whitman nodded. "That's right. Usually, it's a deadbeat dad or someone the courts are looking for to serve papers. I stay away from anything that sounds too hazardous."

"What can you tell us about the case you did for Tawana Williams?" Marshall asked.

Whitman pushed a file folder over to Crowley "Usually I try to maintain client confidentiality. But seeing as she's dead, there is no real need. Besides, I understand this is a homicide investigation. Not that I had any special fondness for Ms. Williams. I mean she was a nice person and I hate to see any killer get away with murder. Anyway, Ms. Williams asked me to locate a man named Donald Belanger. Took me almost an hour on the computer to get his address and phone number. Also found out he used to be a state game warden. Retired after thirty-eight years. I drove out to the guy's house and confirmed he still lived there. I followed him to Walmart. I called the phone number I had for him, and he answered. After that, I told Ms. Williams what I had found, and she paid me five hundred dollars. The info is in the file."

Marshall examined the contents of the file before passing it to Freedman. Marshall pointed out one of the phone numbers in the file. It was the disconnected phone number Freedman had tried earlier.

"Now don't think I'm questioning your investigation," Whitman said. "But this guy is over sixty and seems like a decent guy. So, what does he have to do with your case?"

"I noticed he lives alone and has never been married," Freedman commented.

"True." Whitman replied. "Again, I was asked to find the guy, not to do a background check."

"Have you had any contact with him since Ms. Williams asked you to find him?" Marshall asked.

Whitman shook his head. "Nope. But Ms. Williams also asked me to locate a second person. Turns out it was a reporter, Becky Watson, who was shot a couple of weeks ago."

"Why was that?" Marshall asked.

"Don't really know. However, Williams left instructions I was to mail a package to that reporter. That's what I did. Then a week later, I read about Williams' death. Strange thing was I heard the reporter was shot too." Don't know if the reporter got it or not, but I did mail it."

"Do you know what was in the package?"

Whitman shook his head. "No idea, but I'm willing to bet it's what got Williams killed and that reporter shot."

Freedman closed the file. "We'll check to see if she got it. We appreciate your assistance with this. I hate to use the old line that we are not allowed to comment on any open investigations. So, I hope you understand."

Whitman nodded. "Not a problem. If that helps you find Ms. Williams' killer, then I'm glad to help. Still, once the case is closed, wouldn't mind if you stopped by and let me know what happened. If it makes you more comfortable, we could meet for a couple of beers and swap war stories."

Marshall stood up and shook Whitman's hand. "Look forward to it."

∞∞∞∞∞∞

He recognized them as cops even before they parked their car. He wasn't happy to see them. He waited until they rang his doorbell before answering the door. He glared at them. "What do you want?"

Freedman smiled at him. "I would love a medium rare steak with a nice bottle of wine, although I will settle for a cold beer. But that's not why we're here."

"Not funny."

Marshall pulled out his badge. "I know. I keep telling him he has no chance at a career as a comedian, but he doesn't listen to me. I'm Detective Marshall and this is my partner, Detective Freedman. Mind if we come in. We'd like to ask you a few questions."

"Yeah, I knew you were cops. So, what do you want?"

"Need to ask you a few questions," Marshall answered.

"About what?"

Freedman faced Marshall. "Let me try." He took a step forward and placed his hand on the screen door. "We're investigating a homicide and think you may be able to help us. Now, we know you used to work for the state as a game warden, so you know how we, the police, operate. So why don't you cooperate?"

He stared at Freedman, then Marshall. "All right. What do you need to know?"

"That's better," Freedman replied. "Let's start with seeing some identification."

"Stay there," he said, "I'll go and get it."

He left the doorway and retreated into the house. Marshall pulled his weapon and moved to one side of the doorway. Freedman did the same, moving to the opposite side.

"Relax," he bellowed as he returned. "I'm not going to shoot you. Here, here's my driver's license." Belanger opened the screen door and extended to Freedman.

Freedman holstered his weapon and took Belanger's driver's license. After a brief, but thorough examination, he returned it to him. "Thank you, Mr. Belanger. Just needed to confirm your identity." Marshall also holstered his weapon but remained standing to one side of the screen door.

"Yeah, yeah, I know all that."

"As Detective Marshall stated earlier, we need to ask you a few questions. We are conducting a homicide investigation. The victim was Ms. Tawana Williams. I believe you know her?"

"Never heard of the woman," Belanger replied.

"It seems she knew you," Freedman commented. "We have phone records showing she called your phone number."

"Really? When did she call? I don't remember anyone by that name calling me. Maybe she was one of those women calling to get me to buy an extended auto warranty for my car."

Freedman pulled out the phone listing from the file Whitman had given them. "Don't think so." He pointed to a number on the paper. "Isn't that your phone number?"

Belanger took the phone listing from Freedman. He looked closely at it for a few seconds before handing it back to the detective. "That's an old phone. I lost it weeks ago. Probably whoever found it called her. But it wasn't me. I don't know this person."

"She hired a private investigator to find you," Marshall stated. "Now why would she do that if she didn't know you?"

"Probably had me mixed up with someone else. Who knows why people do the crazy things they do these days?"

"Your contact with her may have been years ago," Marshall said. "Maybe when you were younger, you sought the services of a prostitute?"

"You're telling me this woman was a hooker? Hell, she's probably hoping to blackmail me into some kind of child support for one of her six kids. Don't know what she wanted. Don't know who she was. And I'm not admitting to being with any hooker, now or ever."

"So, you don't know her. She never called you. You haven't had any contact with her."

"That's right."

"What about a young lady named Becky Watson?" Freedman asked.

"Who's she?"

"She's a woman who was shot a couple of weeks ago," Freedman answered.

"Don't know her," Belanger adamantly stated.

"Wouldn't know a Terry Lambert, would you?" Marshall asked.

"No," Belanger replied. "I don't know anyone who works for a newspaper."

"Okay," Marshall said. "Thank you for your time. "Freedman joined Marshall as he walked back to their car. "Strange," he said with a smile, "You never told him that they worked for a newspaper."

∞∞∞∞∞

Belanger watched the two detectives walk back to their car and leave. He was glad he had gotten rid of the old phone when Tawana Williams was killed. He didn't want to take any chances. He bought a burner phone with cash after that. Still, somehow the police had found him. Also, there was that damn reporter, and who knew what she had told the police.

CHAPTER THIRTY-FIVE

While Marshall and Freedman were busy tracking down Belanger, the day started differently for Oha as he entered the office and placed the box of sweets on the conference table. "I got donuts. I made sure to get you an apple fritter, which you like so much."

"Thanks," Jennifer mumbled without looking up from the files covering the conference table.

Oha went over to the coffee pot and poured himself a cup of coffee. "How long have you been here? I usually beat you into the office in the morning."

"For about two hours."

Oha joined Jennifer at the conference table. He picked up one of the files. "See you're reviewing the cold cases. Any luck?"

"Maybe," Jennifer answered. "Yesterday, I went to interview a potential witness. She described an incident from when she worked the streets. She said a john beat her up when she lit a cigarette. It caused him to start coughing and he had difficulty breathing."

"Okay," Oha said slowly.

"Now take a look at the personal effects found on these victims."

Oha examined the files. Personal effects for the first victim, Marianne Kesler, were a Florida sunshine tee shirt, blue jeans, underwear, and a bra, forty-three cents in change, some Juicy Fruit chewing gum, and a receipt from a convenience store for Chap Stick and a pack of cigarettes. Denise Varney was the second victim, and her personal effects were jeans, a brown blouse, underwear, a ballpoint pen, a matchbook, and a receipt from a convenience store for candy bars. The third victim was Kathleen Luprio, whose effects were a green dress, a pair of sandals, a white bra and panties, a Bic lighter, and a roach clip. The personal effects of the last victim, Theresa Hallman, included a black skirt, a white blouse, a white bra and panties, a pair of tennis shoes, and half a pack of cigarettes.

"Notice anything?" Jennifer asked Oha.

"None of the victims had any ID, and two of them were missing their shoes."

"I'm betting they were all smokers. One of them had matches, one a lighter, one a receipt for cigarettes, and one had half a pack of cigarettes."

"Did you check their autopsy reports to see if they were?"

Jennifer pointed to the clock on the wall. "The medical examiner's office doesn't open till nine. As soon as they do, I'll give them a call."

"So, you think we have a psychopath killing smokers. Seems like he would have surfaced long before now. How can anyone get away with killing cigarette smokers for thirty-some years?"

"According to the person I interviewed yesterday, the guy picked up prostitutes. If they smoked while they were with the john, he started having breathing problems and became violent."

"Well, we can't search the records of every person we arrested for using the services of a prostitute. Going back thirty years will take forever."

"You're right about that," Jennifer stated. "Furthermore, we don't have the victims' medical history."

"Then how does this help us?"

"Gives us a motive. If smoking caused a severe physical reaction, which caused the person to lose his temper, we now know why he killed his victims."

"Don't buy it," Oha responded. "Doesn't explain why he would now kill someone who was a hooker twenty years ago, shoot a newspaper reporter, and beat up another reporter."

"I believe those three people are the key to revealing who this killer is."

Oha picked up a donut and waved it at Jennifer. "If that's the case, those two reporters are in danger."

∞∞∞∞∞∞

Terry felt a shiver down his back as he entered the building. It was the first time he had entered the county morgue in five years. Paula, standing next to Terry, placed her hand on his shoulder, startling Terry.

"Relax," she said. "There is nothing to worry about."

"But why are we here?" Terry asked. "We don't have to identify anyone who died, do we?"

"Not that I know of," Paula answered as she pointed to Detectives Gunn and Oha, who had entered the building. "We're here to meet them."

Paula's comment piqued Jennifer's curiosity. "We didn't ask you to come here."

"Detective Marshall told us you had a development in the case, and you were coming here to check it out," Paula replied.

"When did he tell you that?" Jennifer asked. "And why did he call you to tell you about our progress with the case?"

Paula grinned. "He told me when I called him this morning and asked about what was happening with the case."

"I see I'm going to have to have a conversation with Detective Marshall," Jennifer said with a degree of contempt.

"Hey," Terry interjected. "Let's not worry about that. Let's just do what we have to do and get out of here. This place gives me the creeps."

"I take it you haven't spent a lot of time around dead bodies," Oha said with a small chuckle.

Terry glared at Oha. "The last time I was here was five years ago when I had to identify my wife, who was killed by a drunk driver. So, forgive me if I don't have any fond memories of the place."

Jennifer stepped between Terry and Oha. Facing Terry she said. "We are here to check up on something from the coroner's files. We don't have to deal with any dead bodies."

Oha stepped aside of Jennifer and nodded to Terry. "Sorry about your wife. I didn't mean to upset you."

Jennifer put her hands on Terry's shoulders. "I know what you're going through. Each person down here had a husband, or a wife, or a father, or a mother, etc. They were loved by their family; a family that is grieving. It's not a pleasant place. As police officers, we develop a wall to help us deal with what goes on here. Sometimes we forget we also need to deal with the living as well as the dead."

"I'm sure Terry understands," Paula said as she gently patted his back. "But could you tell us about this new lead you have on the cases?"

"Come on," Jennifer said with a wave on her hand as she led them to the records office.

"Good morning," a middle-aged woman wearing a tan polo shirt and jeans said as the group entered the office. "What can I do for you today?"

Jennifer handed the woman a piece of paper. "We would like to look at some autopsy reports from cold cases about twenty or thirty years ago. Any chance you could get them for us?"

The receptionist looked at the paper and smiled. "You are in luck. We had a couple of interns here last summer and they got all our old reports scanned into our computer files. It will take me a while to get you copies of these cases. You all can wait in the lounge down the hall while I get them."

Jennifer led the group to the lounge. They all sat down except for Terry who kept pacing around the room, stopping every few minutes to stare out of a window.

Jennifer patted the chair next to her. "Terry, why don't you come here and sit down?"

"Don't want to," Terry answered.

"Not asking," Jennifer said. "I need to ask you some questions. And it's hard if you are walking around. So, come and sit down."

Terry came over and sat down. "What do you want to know?"

"Why don't you tell me about your wife? What was her name?"

Terry took a moment to calm down. "Kristen. I met her when we were in college. She saw me as a person, not as some freak."

"Well, I agree with her. I can see what she saw in you. How long were you married?" Jennifer asked.

"She was killed a few weeks before our eighth wedding anniversary. Can we change the subject?"

"Sure. Tell me what you found out about these cases so far," Jennifer asked.

"Nothing much. Paula and I even went out to the store where the first victim was last seen. Dead end. The store is still there, but the owner who was there thirty years ago is long gone. Turns out the place is nothing like it was then. There used to be a couple of trailer parks and some kind of commune. They tore down the trailer parks and built houses. The commune is long gone, moved to another place. But I told you all this last night at dinner."

Paula's ears perked up, not at the mention of her name but that of Terry and Jennifer having dinner together last night. "That's true. Becky, our friend who was shot, went out there and didn't find anything either."

"When did she go out there?" Jennifer asked.

"The weekend before she was shot," Paula answered.

"But Paula and I went out there," Terry added. "We didn't find anything out there relating to the murder, especially since it happened so long ago."

"You missed the point," Jennifer said. "The evidence you need to look at isn't what happened thirty years ago. The evidence you need to find happened the Sunday when your friend visited that store."

The receptionist returned with the files. It took Jennifer less than twenty minutes to confirm her suspicions. They now had a motive for murdering all those women.

CHAPTER THIRTY-SIX

"Well, we're back," Terry said as Paula pulled up to Stranden's Convenience Store. "Do you really think we're going to find anything here?"

Paula turned off the ignition and motioned toward the store. "Maybe. I'm just hoping they still have the surveillance records from when Becky was out here. It's been almost a month."

"Do you think they will give it to us?" Terry asked.

"Let's find out." Paula got out of her car. Terry followed her into the store.

The owner came out of the back room when the chime rang as Paula and Terry entered the store. "Good afternoon," he said trying to hide his foreign accent, "Good to see you again."

"Thank you," Paula responded. "I'm hoping you can help us."

"Of course," the owner said.

Terry pulled out a photograph and pointed to Becky in the picture. "Have you seen this woman? She would have been in here several weeks ago."

The owner looked at the photo. "Sorry, I can't say. I don't recognize her, but she may have come in. Unless they are regular, I don't remember people very well."

"Of course not," Paula replied. "But do you have surveillance records for the last month?"

"Why you ask?" the owner said with anxiety in his voice.

"If you do," Paula continued, "perhaps you could show them to us."

The owner shook his head and waved his hand. "No. No. I must respect privacy of my customer. I cannot show them to anyone who come to my store. Sorry, no, no."

Paula held up her hand to calm the owner down. "I understand your position. But a friend of ours was shot a couple of weeks ago and we think maybe the person who did it is on one of your surveillance files. It would really be helpful if we could see them."

"No. No. No." The owner insisted. "If this important, then police come here. They haven't come, so no record."

Paula, Terry, and the owner stared at each other for a moment. "Okay," Paula said. "It's okay. But if you have them, please do not delete them. Those files may be the answer to several murders that happened years ago."

"If police come, I give them the file. But not you."

"Well, then I have good news for you," a voice behind Paula and Terry said. "I'm Detective Gunn and this is my partner, Detective Oha."

While looking at the owner, Jennifer pulled out a piece of paper and placed it on the counter. "This is a search warrant. Let's talk."

∞∞∞∞∞∞

Once they were back in Jennifer's office, she placed the recordings from the store in her computer. Oha, Paula, and Terry watched the monitor from behind Jennifer. The image of the inside of Stranden's Convenience Store appeared on the monitor. Jennifer fast forwarded until they saw Becky come on the screen. Twice they watched the film thirty minutes before Becky entered the store and for thirty minutes after she left.

"Besides Becky, there weren't that many customers," Terry commented.

"More importantly, the only person who fit the profile of our killer was an old man with one leg and using crutches," Jennifer added.

Paula tapped Jennifer on the shoulder. "How about seeing if there is anything on the outside cameras?"

Jennifer switched the camera files. Again, she fast forwarded the footage until Becky arrived. Jennifer rewound the file thirty minutes before Becky arrived. The four spectators watched the screen until Becky got into her car and left. Less than a minute later, a dark Cadillac

SUV appeared on the screen. It stopped briefly before leaving the parking lot.

"Stop," Paula demanded. "Back it up. I want to see that car again."

Jennifer complied. "What do you see?"

"That car," Paula answered. "That car could be something."

"Why is that?" Oha inquired.

Paula pointed to the car on the screen. "I stopped by Becky's place after she was shot. I talked to a neighbor of hers. She said the car was a dark SUV with strange taillights, shaped like parenthesis, just like that car."

"And you think this is the same car," Jennifer replied. "It could be a possibility."

"Yes," shouted Terry. "You can run the license plate and find out who it is."

Jennifer smiled. "I love your enthusiasm. What you didn't notice was the license plate was covered."

"I guess that means there is no way to find out who the driver was." Terry said with disappointment.

"Not necessarily," Jennifer said as she picked up the phone. "Let me see if Detectives Marshall and Freedman can help us."

Marshall and Freedman entered the room two minutes later. "Well, I see you brought everyone together for this special occasion," Marshall said. "What do you have for us?"

Jennifer pointed to her computer monitor. "Hopefully, we've found a lead for my cold cases and your homicide. This is surveillance footage of Ms. Becky Watson visiting Stranden's Convenience Store the Sunday before she was shot. This was the place two of our cold-case victims were last seen alive. Granted, it was years ago, but the place is pretty much the same now as it was then, The view of the inside of the store didn't show anything; but when we watched the view of the outside, we noticed something. There is a black SUV that looks like it followed Ms. Watson."

"Witnesses did say they saw a black SUV leaving the scene after Ms. Watson was shot," Freedman stated.

Jennifer paused the video on the back of the SUV. Paula pointed to the taillights. "I talked to a neighbor after Becky was shot. She said the car had strange taillights, shaped like parenthesis. As you can see, the taillights on this SUV fit that description."

"Now, what do have for us?" Jennifer asked.

"A suspect," Marshall replied. "We found a second phone at our homicide victim's apartment. We checked the phone records. It led us to a private detective. He was hired by our victim to find a Mr. Donald Belanger. Turns out our victim called him. When we questioned him, he denied getting any phone call from our victim. He denied knowing Ms. Becky Watson or Terry, but he did know that they worked for a newspaper. I'm thinking he's our killer."

"Got anything to back it up?" Jennifer asked.

"Nothing at the moment," Marshall answered. "But with what Ms. Stanford just told me, we may have something. I'll check with the DMV and see what kind of car Belanger drives. How about you? Do you have any physical evidence that can tie him to any of your cold cases?"

Jennifer gave Marshall a smirk. "Got some DNA samples. If we can get a DNA sample from him, we can compare them. But I can tell you, you're going to need more than he drives a black SUV to get a warrant for DNA."

"I can get you a DNA sample," Paula interjected.

"NO! You won't," Jennifer commanded. "If you get anything, any evidence at all, it will get thrown out of court when it comes to the chain of custody."

"No, it's easy," Terry stated. "All you have to do is bring him in for questioning, give him a soda or a cup of coffee, and when he leaves, you take the soda or cup and run his DNA."

Jennifer nodded. "That's a good idea; but what do we do if it doesn't work? What if he doesn't drink anything, or takes the drink with him? Also, Detectives Marshall and Freedman already talked to him. Why would he come in for questioning? We need something more than he drives a black SUV with unusual taillights."

"And what if he doesn't own a black SUV," Freedman added. "When we visited him, there was a grey pickup truck in the driveway. I doubt he owes two cars."

"We'll check anyway," Marshall said waving at the photo on the computer.

Paula let out a sigh. "Meanwhile, I'll work on Plan B."

"Please don't," Marshall responded. "Your Plan B tends to get someone shot."

∞∞∞∞∞∞

Belanger didn't like it. The detectives were asking questions about that dead hooker. He knew they would never buy the story of him losing the phone. It didn't matter. If that was their only connection, they had nothing to go on. *But there still was that young reporter. What did she have? Did she have something that could tie him to those killings so long ago. Who knows. He couldn't take the chance, especially after he found that package in her apartment.* He went back to his computer to check on the locator. It was downtown, near medical centers. *Was the blond reporter back in the hospital? It would make it easier to kill her. Or were they down there checking on something else? Where was that woman?*

∞∞∞∞∞∞

Three weeks ago, Cindy Doss was a married woman living in a suburban home, running her kids to soccer practice and other after school activities. She was staring at photographs of her children. She kept shaking, afraid of what had happened that night so long ago. Would that man find her and come back to finish what he had started those many years ago. She thought the danger was long gone, until those articles appeared in newspaper. But she was wrong. Someone had been in her home since that detective and reporter visited her. She could tell by the way things were slightly out of place. Someone had been looking at her children's photos. The files of their home records had been searched. If something was missing, she couldn't tell; but she knew someone had been in her house. Someone was interested in her and her family. Cindy Doss put away the photos of her children. She was not going to be afraid anymore. She was not going to allow anyone to harm her family.

CHAPTER THIRTY-SEVEN
[day thirteen]

"I can't believe we're back here again," Freedman complained as he and Marshall entered Tawana Williams' apartment. "What a way to start the day."

"You had your coffee and donuts. You should be happy."

The apartment still smelled of decomp. Freedman went over and opened a window. He put a small fan near it to blow the air out of the apartment. He leaned against the wall, waiting for Marshall to say something.

Marshall walked slowly around the room before going into the kitchen, then the bedroom and the rest of the apartment. He returned to the living room.

"Find anything?" Freedman asked.

"Haven't started looking."

Freedman closed his eyes, put one hand to his forehead and extended the other one, sweeping it around in front of him.

"What are you doing?" Marshall inquired.

"I'm thinking if I were evidence, where would I hide."

"Give it up," Marshall answered. "The evidence isn't here."

"How do you know?"

"The apartment wasn't tossed. Whoever killed Ms. Williams didn't search the apartment for any evidence, which means either she gave it to him or told him where it was."

"So why are we here?"

"Remember I told you I would check to see what kind of car Belanger had."

Freedman nodded. "Yeah."

"He has a gray pickup truck, which we saw when we went out to talk to him."

"Okay,"

Marshall smiled. "But Ms. Williams drove a black Cadillac SUV. So, where are her car keys?"

∞∞∞∞∞∞

Man, I am getting lazy, Paula thought as she sipped her morning coffee at one of the tables outside of Le Rue. Next to Paula, Keiko kept a watchful eye on the people walking by. She was the first to notice the woman with the dark hair coming toward them. The woman stopped on the other side of the railing separating the outside tables from the rest of the sidewalk.

Paula looked up at the woman.

"I hope you remember me," she said. "We met the other day. I'm Cindy Doss. Your reporter friend interviewed me about a story she was working on."

Paula stood up. "Yes, I remember you. What can I do for you?"

Cindy motioned toward the chair. "Do you mind if I join you?"

"Not at all."

"How about your dog? Does he bite?"

"Keiko's a she, and she won't bother you unless you have some food, which she will try to share with you."

Cindy smiled. "Just give me a minute." Cindy left to enter Le Rue. A few minutes later she came out with a cup of coffee and a muffin. "I brought a bran muffin. I figured it was the best thing they had that I could share."

Paula sat down and invited Cindy to join her. Cindy broke the muffin in half and gave Keiko some, which she greedily wolfed down.

"Well, it's nice to see you again," Paula said. "What can I do for you? Do you have more information about the person who attacked you that night?"

Cindy took a sip of coffee and a moment to gather her nerve. She put down her coffee and cleared her throat. "Actually, I was hoping to talk to that reporter friend of yours. I called the newspaper, and they said she was out sick. They wouldn't give me any other information. I just happened to see you here and thought maybe you could help me."

"Well, I can certainly bring her back out to your house. When would be convenient?"

"No. That's not a good idea."

"Why?" Paula asked.

"Because of what happened to Sweet Tea."

"Sweet Tea?"

"Tawana. Her street name was Sweet Tea."

"Still not following you."

Cindy played with the strap on her purse. "Tawana Williams. She was killed a few weeks ago. She and I were attacked by the same man. And now I find out he may have killed others, even Tawana. If he came after Tawana after all these years, what is to keep him from coming after me? Also, I think someone has been in my house. I was picking up my kids from school. When I got back, I found things moved around, not a lot, just not in the same place, kind of being moved a few inches or so."

"And you're scared," Paula answered.

"Yes, I'm scared. I'm scared he will come after me. I'm scared he will hurt my family. I'm scared that after all these years, my past is going to come back and ruin my life."

"And you're tired of being scared."

"How did you know?" Cindy asked.

"Saw it a lot when I was with the Marines. You're scared, then you get angry at yourself, and that anger turns into hatred of yourself and the enemy. First, we need to focus on protecting your family."

"Already did that. I told my husband about you and that detective visiting me and the feeling someone may have been in our house. He's taken the children with him to his parents' house. They're thrilled to be out of school and to visit their grandparents. Meanwhile, we have our neighbors watching our house in case anyone tries to break in. But I don't know how long this will last and what to do."

"In your case, there's good news."

"There is?"

"Yeah, there is. I know a couple of cops who are going to make sure you and your family are safe."

"I don't want the cops or this guy anywhere near my family."

Paula nodded that she understood. "Finish your coffee. Then we'll see what we can do."

∞∞∞∞∞∞

Belanger followed the tracker to this coffee shop. He watched as that tall blond walked her dog into the shop and came out to sit at one of the outside tables. He sat in his truck, hoping no one would demand he move out of the parking space. He kept scanning both sides of the street, hoping to see that young blond reporter when he noticed a woman with dark hair come up and start talking to the tall blond. After a brief exchange, the woman went into the coffee shop and came out after a few minutes and sat down with the tall blond. He noticed the woman gave the dog some of her muffin. Belanger knew this woman. He had been in her house searching for any evidence of their encounter years ago. Her being there was not a coincidence.

CHAPTER THIRTY-EIGHT

Terry was staring at his computer screen when Diana came over and sat down next to him. "What are you doing?" she asked.

"Just going over the files on the victims that Jennifer showed us."

"You mean the ones we got from the pretty detective that Marshall and Freedman introduced us to?" Diana asked in a melonic voice.

"Yes," Terry acknowledged. "The thing that is puzzling is the last murder happened more than fifteen years ago. And now he has resurfaced. Why was the killer gone for fifteen years?"

Diana leaned back in her chair, putting her hand to her chin. She took a moment before responding. "My first thought is maybe the killer was in prison."

"I doubt that," Terry replied. "Jennifer said she had DNA samples from the crime scenes. If he was in prison, they would have his DNA and be able to match it."

"Maybe he got religion."

"Possible, but then why start killing again? Even if he lost religion, I doubt he would revert to killing. No there was a reason he stopped."

"Well, I'm out of ideas," Diana said as she twirled her chair and stood up. "Do you have anything?"

"Maybe, but it's just a guess. I doubt there is any way we can find out if it's anything."

"What's your idea?"

Terry looked up at Diana. "What if he stopped for some medical reason?"

∞∞∞∞∞∞

Paula pulled her car out of the parking lot after Cindy parked her car on a side street next to a public park. Cindy was in the passenger seat and Keiko in the back. Paula turned onto the street. She noticed a black Cadillac SUV two cars ahead of her. It had the taillights Becky's neighbor had described. At the next traffic light, the Cadillac went straight. Paula turned right without signaling her intent. A few moments later, she noticed a black SUV behind her. After traveling a few miles down the road, Paula pulled into a Walmart shopping center. She was unable to see if the black SUV followed her, but she did notice another black Cadillac SUV in a handicapped parking spot. Paula drove through the parking lot, exiting onto a side street. She made a point to meander through side streets for about ten minutes before returning to a main street and her way to the police station. A few minutes later, Paula noticed a black SUV about five cars behind her. She moved to the left lane. She watched to see if the black SUV would follow her.

"What are you doing?" Cindy asked.

"Seeing if we're being followed," Paula answered.

"Someone's following us!"

"Not sure. You remember Becky, the woman who brought us to your house?"

"Yeah."

"She was shot a couple of weeks ago. One of the neighbors described a black SUV with strange taillights. So far, I've noticed several black SUVs."

"You mean there's a conspiracy, a group of people out to kill me?"

Paula chuckled. "I think it's a case of my noticing black SUVs more than I did before. I've seen it before. You start to see an enemy everywhere."

"But how do you know that one of them isn't really a threat?"

Paula glanced at Cindy before answering. "You don't, and that's the problem."

∞∞∞∞∞∞

"Where the hell are they going," Belanger said to himself. Following the tall blond and the other woman was easy until they got to the Walmart parking lot, but once they left, going onto a side street, he realized they were aware of being followed. He remained in the Walmart parking lot, watching the tracker as the two women meandered through side streets. They turned back onto a major road. Belanger left the parking lot but remained out of sight. As long as he had the tracker, he didn't need to follow them too closely.

CHAPTER THIRTY-NINE

"I brought lunch," Marshall said as he and Freedman walked into Jennifer's and Oha's office. "Hope you like Chinese."

"Grew up on it," Oha answered. "What's the occasion?"

"We need to talk," Marshall replied, pulling out containers from a paper bag. "We're looking at Donald Belanger, but he drives a gray pickup truck. He doesn't and has never owned a black SUV. David and I met up with a private detective Tawana Williams hired. She wanted to locate her old pimp, who is in prison, and Mr. Donald Belanger. We found a second phone belonging to Williams and turns out she called Belanger. He claims he lost the phone and never heard from her. He said he didn't know her or Ms. Watson. It looked like a dead end, except Tawana Williams had a black Cadillac SUV, which happens to have the kind of taillights Ms. Stanford told us about. David and I went back to William's apartment and searched for the keys. We couldn't find them. We're thinking Belanger took Williams' car and used it when he shot the reporter."

Jennifer pulled out some paper plates from a cupboard and scooped rice onto them. "So, we're looking for a black Caddy with weird taillights, but the prime suspect drives a pickup."

The others helped themselves to whatever was in the cartons. "We're put a BOLO for Tawana Williams' car," Freedman added.

"The question is where can Belanger hide a black SUV?" Marshall stated. "We're running a check on any properties he might own. So far, it's his home and a storage unit, which is too small for a car."

Oha waved a plastic fork at Marshall. "What about family, brothers, sisters, etc. Do we have their names and addresses?"

Freedman nodded. "According to our records, he's single and never been married. His closest relative is a sister living in Colorado."

"He would need a secure place to store the car," Jennifer stated. "Some place not connected to him or anyone close to him. Also, a place that could hold his pickup truck at the same time while he changes vehicles. Some place like a parking garage that is open 24 hours a day. Some place where it could remain for several days without attracting attention."

"You mean some place like the parking lot at the airport," Freedman said.

"No," Jennifer responded. "That would leave a record of him going in and leaving. That also excludes any parking garages that charge any kind of fee. And a parking lot like Walmart's wouldn't work either. It would only be a matter of time before some employee would notice it's always in the same spot and not moving."

"So, where do you hide a car that you want no one to find?" Oha asked.

Jennifer pointed her finger at Oha. "Somewhere in plain sight."

∞∞∞∞∞∞

Jennifer hated it when others expected her to assume the typical female role of cleaning up after a meal. So, she made sure the other three detectives did it when they finished lunch. She did make sure any leftovers were stored in the refrigerator for later.

"I'm glad you came in," Jennifer said to Marshall and Freedman when they finished cleaning up. "Detective Oha and I stopped by the coroner's office yesterday and asked for them to check something for me. They were able to pull the autopsy records for our cold case victims, both here and in Park Hills. All the victims were smokers."

"Well, that tells us something they had in common," Marshall replied. "But I hardly think the motive in these cases is our killer hates people who smoke."

Jennifer nodded in agreement. "Also, two days ago, I interviewed a woman who was a victim of an attack years ago. The perpetrator of that attack fits the profile of the murderer of these women. She stated that when she lit a cigarette, he started coughing, sneezing, and farting. She said it was funny, but when she started laughing, he started beating her. Fortunately, another guest at the hotel where this took place started banging on the door. It interrupted the attack. The john left, but she was savagely beaten. So, what if the motive was an angry reaction to being laughed at when he went into one of these coughing fits? All our victims were beaten and strangled, which leads me to think none of the murders were premeditated. But then, the way they were killed led me to believe that anyway."

"So, you think our killer and this individual who lost it are the same person," Marshall responded. "Pretty thin."

Jennifer smiled. "I failed to mention one thing. This woman was interviewed by Becky Watson, who was shot for looking into these cold cases. Also, this woman said she used to know Tawana Williams. A homicide you're working on with a connection to your suspect."

"It's definitely possible they're all connected," Marshall added. "The private investigator we talked to said he was asked to locate Becky Watson, the reporter who was shot. He told us Williams instructed him to send a package to Watson."

"Did she get it?" Jennifer asked.

Marshall shrugged his shoulders. "Haven't had a chance to ask her yet."

"Please check to see if she did. Meanwhile, remember Terry Lambert and the night he was attacked?" Jennifer inquired of the others. They nodded that they did.

"He described his assailant as an older man, about medium build, and fairly tall." Jennifer looked at Marshall and Freedman. "How would you describe Donald Belanger?"

"Fairly tall, medium build, in his sixties," Freedman answered.

"He fits the description," Oha responded.

Marshall nodded in agreement. "What we need to do is find that missing car."

CHAPTER FORTY

This is getting old," Belanger said to himself. *I don't need to follow these two. I need to find that blond reporter. I need to know what she found out.* Belanger pulled into the parking lot of a small strip mall. He watched the tracker on his computer screen. The signal kept moving. He realized following these two would lead nowhere. *That's it,* Belanger thought. *I'm going home. I have a better idea.*

∞∞∞∞∞

Cindy looked out the back window every few minutes, searching for black cars. Keiko assumed it meant Cindy wanted to pet her, which made it harder to spot anyone tailing them. It's hard to see around a German shepherd begging for attention when it's taking up the back seat.

"Relax," Paula said as she pulled on Cindy's arm to pry her away from Keiko. "You're getting my dog all excited. If there's someone following us, I know one sure way to find out."

"What's that?" Cindy asked.

"We'll go to the police station. If we are being followed, as soon as he realizes where we're going, he'll peel off. That will give us a chance to see who it is."

"But he'll be behind us."

"Either he will pass us or turn. If he turns, we'll turn around and follow him. With luck we can get his license plate number and the cops can track him down."

Cindy looked out the passenger window before looking back again and facing Paula. "What if he has a gun? What if he starts shooting at us?"

Paula pointed to the glove box. "Open that up.'

Cindy complied and gasped when she saw the nine-millimeter, automatic pistol. "What are you doing with a gun?"

"It's called being prepared in case he does start shooting And don't worry. I'm a damn good shot."

"I don't like guns."

Paula reached over and took the pistol from the glove box. She placed it in the side pocket of the driver's door. "You don't have to like them. If shooting starts, duck down below the dashboard."

"What if he shoots you first?"

"Then run like hell."

∞∞∞∞∞

Bill Fitch came out of his office and walked over to where Diana was talking to Terry. "What's up?" he asked.

"Just trying to figure out why this guy quit killing fifteen years ago, and why he started up again now," Terry answered. "Any ideas?"

Fitch shrugged his shoulders. "Prison, religion, moved out of state, I don't know."

"Doubt it was any of those," Diana replied. "Terry thinks it might have been medical."

Fitch chuckled. "Good luck with that. No doctor is going to discuss any patients with you."

"What if we ask the pharmacies or rehab clinics?" Terry suggested.

"Nope," Fitch stated. "They are bound by the HIPAA (Health Insurance Portability and Accountability Act) Laws doctors need to obey. They aren't going to give you any information."

"So, it's a dead end." Terry responded with a sigh.

"No, it's not," Diana contradicted. "It's an idea that might help us catch the killer. I don't know how, but it just might."

"You're forgetting something," Fitch pointed out. "The real issue isn't why he stopped killing years ago. It's why is he killing people now."

∞∞∞∞∞

Paula made it a point to note each car that passed her and Cindy as they sat in Paula's car in the police station parking lot. They waited for several minutes before Paula put her pistol back in the glove box.

"I don't want the police involved," Cindy pleaded. "This guy might be a cop."

Paula shook her head. "I doubt it. If he was a cop, he would have chased you down when he beat you up. He could have easily gone into the hospital and got your information. Furthermore, you're married, with a different name. But most importantly, I'm taking you to people I trust. I've dealt with them before. And, they have an interest in catching this guy who beat you and killed your friend. So, relax. It'll be okay. Come on, let's go."

Paula got out and opened the rear door for Keiko. Cindy hesitantly got out. She stood still and looked around, checking, searching for anyone who was watching her. Paula came around the car with Keiko. "You've got nothing to fear," Paula said to calm Cindy. "Between me and Keiko, no one is going to bother you. Besides, we haven't seen anything suspicious for a while. No one followed us here."

∞∞∞∞∞

Belanger set up his computer on the coffee table in front of his recliner. He went into the kitchen and found a notepad and pen. He sat in his recliner and started writing. He made a list of the places where the tracker showed the tall blond had stopped. He knew that one of those places was where the blond reporter was staying. He noticed the tracker was stationary.

A quick look on his computer map app showed their current location. *What are they doing back at the police station?* he thought. He considered driving by to make sure they were there but decided against it. With the signal from the tracker, there was no need. Also, he didn't want to risk being seen or photographed by any security cameras. He would need to wait a little longer before he could find that blond reporter and kill her.

∞∞∞∞∞∞

A patrol officer knocked on the door of Marshall's and Freedman's office. He opened the door to let Paula, Keiko, and Cindy in. Marshall nodded to let the officer know it was okay and that he could leave.

Marshall motioned for Paula and Cindy to have a seat. "What brings you here?" Keiko nuzzled Marshall before settling down on the floor next to Paula.

Paula placed her hand on Cindy's shoulder. "Cindy here is concerned about the cases you and Becky are investigating. She thinks that the killer will come after her, or worse, her family."

Freedman came over to join the conversation. He extended his hand to Cindy. "I'm Detective David Freedman, Detective Marshall's partner. Perhaps you could tell us why you feel you're in danger?"

"Sorry about that," Marshall said. "I should introduce myself too. I'm Detective Nick Marshall. But we work homicide. The cold cases you are referring to are handled by Detectives Gunn and Oha. They're upstairs.

Paula shook her head. "No, you're the ones we want to talk to. Ms. Cindy Doss used to be a prostitute and was a victim of an attack that fits the profile of your killer. That was many years ago. She left that life and is now a homemaker, wife, mother, and concerned citizen. She was also one of the people interviewed by Becky. And she knew Ms. Tawana Williams, the homicide you are working on."

"Okay," Freedman replied slowly while looking at Cindy. "So, why do you feel you're in danger? Have you had any contact with the person who attacked you back then?"

"No," Cindy answered. "But Sweet Tea, I'm sorry, I mean Tawana Williams, was killed. We worked the streets at the same time and I'm sure the same person attacked both of us. Also, I think he may have been in my house. One time when I picked up my children from school, after I got home, I noticed things were moved around, like someone had gone through things before putting them back, but not in the exact place they were in before. He might have been looking for something to connect me to Sweet Tea. If he killed her, then he'll want to kill me too."

Marshall nodded and held up his hand. "Excuse me for a few minutes. I'll be right back.

Freedman waited until Marshall left the office before facing Cindy. "I understand you being concerned and even a bit afraid, but I doubt you have anything to worry about. Were you and Ms. Williams close?"

"No, we weren't," Cindy replied. "Once I left that lifestyle, I didn't associate with any of the other girls. Not that I'm a snob. It's just that I didn't want anything to do with it. In fact, I haven't seen Sweet Tea for years."

Freedman nodded. "Well, while we're waiting for Detective Marshall to return, would you like anything to drink?'

Paula shook her head notifying Freedman she didn't want a drink. Cindy also declined Freedman's offer.

Hoping to get a treat, Keiko watched Freedman when he stood up. "Then you'll excuse me. I'm going to get a cup of coffee." He walked over to the coffee maker on top of a counter in the office. He poured himself a cup, turned and motioned to the two women if they would like some. Again, they both declined. Freedman returned to his desk.

He was desperately searching for a topic of conversation when Marshall returned. He held a folder in his hand.

"I'm sorry," Marshall said as he sat down. "I've forgotten your name."

"It's Cindy Doss."

"Thank you, Ms. Doss. If I understand correctly, this attack you suffered was several years ago. The statute of limitations has expired. But is there any possibility that you could identify the person who attacked you, even though it was years ago?"

Cindy held her head high. "Yes, he put me in the hospital. I will always remember him."

Marshall opened the folder he had in his hand. He laid out six photographs on his desk. "The photos were taken from the drivers' licenses of six men. Let me know if you recognize any of these individuals."

Cindy picked each photo up and looked at it in turn. She placed all six of them back on Marshall's desk, spread them out so he could see all of them. She placed her hand on one photo. "That's the man who beat me up. And I'm sure he's the same man who beat up Sweet Tea when she was working the streets."

Marshall picked up the photo and showed it to Freedman. They now had a suspect.

CHAPTER FORTY-ONE

Terry raised his beer and motioned for Jennifer to join him at the table in the back of Murphy's. "Glad you could make it," he said as Jennifer sat down.

A waitress came over and took Jennifer's drink order. She waited until the waitress left before facing Terry. "Hey, thanks for calling. What did you want to talk about?"

"Diana and I were reviewing the cases you sent to us. There was one thing that puzzled us. Why did this guy stop killing women fifteen years ago, but start killing people now?"

Jennifer drummed the fingers of her right hand on the table while holding her chin with her other hand. "Good point. I figured he was out of the area. I know he wasn't in prison, because if he was, we would have his DNA on file. What did you guys come up with?"

"We're probably wrong," Terry responded while toying with his beer, "what if he stopped because of medical reasons?"

Jennifer tilted her head. "It's possible. What kind of medical problems do you think would cause him to stop killing women?"

Terry shrugged his shoulders. "No idea. But if he wasn't in prison or became religious, there had to be a reason for him stopping."

"Well, I have no idea why he stopped killing women, but we did make some progress."

Terry put down his beer. "Really, what did you find out?"

"Oha and I met with Marshall and Freedman today. They found a person of interest. They believe this guy had some kind of connection to Tawana Williams, a woman who was murdered a couple of weeks ago. According to ballistics, the same gun was used to kill her and shoot your friend, Becky."

"I know. You told me that already. Have they arrested him?"

Jennifer shook her head. "No probable cause or evidence tying him to either shooting."

"What kind of car does this guy drive? Paula told me the person who shot Becky was driving a black SUV."

"We checked. This guy owns a gray pickup truck."

Terry leaned forward and thrusted out his hand for emphasis. "Maybe he owns a second car. Maybe he rented a black SUV. Somehow, he got a black SUV."

"Well, there is one possibility," Jennifer acknowledged. "Tawana Williams, the woman that was murdered, owned a black Cadillac SUV. We haven't been able to locate it. It's possible our suspect was using her car when he shot Becky. But we have no idea where he is hiding it."

∞∞∞∞∞

"What are we doing here?" Cindy asked as Paula pulled into the driveway at Wanda's house.

"A friend lives here," Paula replied. "I want to check on Becky."

"Is this where she lives?" Cindy shouted. "That killer knows where she lives. Didn't he shoot her outside of her home?"

Paula put her hand on Cindy's shoulder. "Relax. Becky was shot outside of her apartment, which isn't here. Becky is staying here, with our friend, kind of hiding out from our killer. We're safe here."

Paula got out of her car and opened the door for Keiko, who bounded out into the yard. She laid down and rubbed her back in the grass before jumping up and returning to Paula. "Are you happy now?" she asked her dog. Keiko responded by wagging her tail.

Cindy chuckled as she joined Paula. "You have a great dog. She's full of energy."

"Wait till you meet Tarzan."

"Tarzan," Cindy queried.

"The owner of the house has a dog named Tarzan. She calls him that 'because he goes ape whenever someone comes over,' so she says."

The door of the house opened and an overweight woman appeared. "Don't just stand there. Come on in."

Paula led Cindy as she and Keiko walked up to the woman. "Cindy, this is Wanda Terrell, owner of the house and lover of animals."

Cindy extended her hand. "Nice to meet you."

"Well, come in," Wanda commanded. "Always happy to have company."

The three women along with Keiko walked through the door and into the living room where Becky was sitting on a sofa. Tarzan jumped off the sofa and ran to greet Keiko and guests.

"Oh, don't mind Tarzan. He goes ape whenever somebody comes over."

Cindy glanced at Paula and giggled a little at their private joke. "I think he's marvelous," Cindy said as she tried to pet the wiggling canine.

"What brings you here?" Becky asked.

"Just wanted to check on you," Paula answered. "Cindy and I spent the day together and stopped by the police station. Cindy identified the man who attacked her that night long ago. Marshall and Freedman think they may have a suspect in those cold cases and who shot you."

"Really, that's great," Becky shouted. "Then they can arrest him and I can go back to my apartment."

"Not quite," Paula replied. "While Cindy can identify him as the person who beat her, the statute of limitations has expired. They need to find evidence linking him to the crimes. Meanwhile, Cindy is staying with me. She doesn't want to place her family in danger."

"And where is she going to sleep?" Wanda demanded with her arms crossed. "You live in a one-bedroom apartment."

Paula turned toward Cindy before answering Wanda. "I figured she could sleep on my couch."

Wanda glared at Paula.

Cindy waved her hand. "That will be fine. I don't mind couch surfing for a few days. I've dealt with worse situations. Besides, I would feel safer staying with someone than being in a hotel."

"Not a problem," Wanda exclaimed, throwing up her hands. "You can stay here. Becky has the guest room, but you are welcome to use the couch right here."

"I couldn't impose," Cindy balked. "Besides, I need to pick up my car."

"Your car is fine," Paula replied. "I'm sure no one will bother it."

"And you're not imposing," Wanda insisted. "The more, the merrier." Wanda pointed to Paula. "And I hope you'll stay too."

Cindy gave Paula a confused look. "If Becky is in the guest room and I'm on the couch, where are you going to sleep?"

Paula grinned at Wanda. "I'll be fine. Besides, the main reason Wanda wants me here is for Keiko and me for guard duty."

Wanda walked over to Paula and gave her a gentle hug. "I always feel safer with an ex-Marine around."

"I'm not an ex-Marine. I'm a former military police officer, but I will always be a Marine."

"Wonderful," Wanda said as she pulled away from Paula. "I feel safer already."

CHAPTER FORTY-TWO

Belanger grabbed a beer and sat down in his recliner. He picked up his computer mouse and activated the computer screen. The tracker was no longer at the police station. Belanger checked the tracker's current location on his computer. It showed the tracker at a home in a modest neighborhood. He cross-referenced the current location with the others he noted earlier. This location was one he plotted twice before. Belanger smiled. He knew where to find that blond reporter and it seemed they were there for the night.

Belanger drove to the home where the tracker was. He found the tall blond's car in front of house. He could hear dogs barking throughout the neighborhood. A quick look around showed there wasn't any place he could remain inconspicuous. He wouldn't be able to kill the reporter tonight. It didn't matter; He had another plan.

∞∞∞∞∞∞

Terry opened the door, allowing Jennifer to exit Murphy's. "Thanks for coming," Terry said as he slowly let the door close.

"My pleasure," Jennifer replied. "Enjoyed the company."

"So did I."

Jennifer crossed her arms and stared at Terry. "You know, the evening is still young. If you're up to it, I'd like to show you something."

Terry blushed. "Thank you and I'm flattered. But I'm not sure I'm ready for anything romantic."

Jennifer chuckled. "Now I'm flattered. However, what I had in mind was to show something related to the case."

"What is it?"

Jennifer turned and motioned for Terry to follow her. "It's at my office." Jennifer smiled. "Don't worry. I promise you I'll behave myself."

This time Terry chuckled. "That's disappointing."

Jennifer pulled out the keys to her car. "Well, I'll try not to be that disappointing."

∞∞∞∞∞∞

Jennifer turned on the lights to her office. Terry hesitated in the doorway for a second before following Jennifer. "Gets kind of spooky here after hours, doesn't it," he said.

Jennifer faced Terry and smiled. "Relax. All the ghosts are downstairs. We keep them locked up."

"Interested in how you do that."

"I knew it," Jennifer said with a chuckle. "Always a newspaper man. Always looking for a story."

Terry shrugged his shoulders. "If you're not going to give me a story, why did you bring me up here?"

Jennifer brought Terry over to her desk and turned on her computer. "Do you know anything about crime analysis?"

"I guess it's the same as other forms of analysis. You're looking for patterns to predict future trends."

Jennifer made a pistol gesture with her hand. "You're spot on. Except in this case, we can't predict future events. Our data is too old. But we were able to determine certain patterns. For instance, the victims were young ladies, all under the age of thirty. They had high-risk lifestyles. The killer always removed any identifying objects such as a driver's license."

"You told me that already," Terry replied with frustration in his voice.

Jennifer pointed to her computer screen that displayed a series of blue and red dots, each with a date. "The blue dots show where we believe the victims were taken. The red ones show where their bodies were found. All the murders took place in the southwestern part of the state. None crossed the state line. Each victim was taken from a location in one county and dumped in another. The killer made sure to cross jurisdiction boundaries. Furthermore, he made sure to dump the bodies at least two counties away, making it more difficult for police agencies to tie the crimes together. That, and the time between each homicide kept anyone from realizing we were dealing with a serial killer."

"Why didn't the FBI know this?"

"The crimes were too spread out, both geographically and chronologically."

Terry shook his head. "But you found several of the bodies here in this county. You investigate cold cases. Surely, you must have seen the connection."

Jennifer took a deep breath. "It's not that easy. There are dozens of Jane Doe cases and many more homicides. While I do make it a point to review cold cases at least once a year, I have current cases I work on. I review the cases when things are slow, which means I may review one case one week and another two weeks later. When I review the cases, I look at them individually, not as a group. That's why it's so easy for me or Detective Oha to miss these patterns."

"But Becky found them."

"Yes, she did. And I'm glad she did. But remember, she was looking for a pattern and she reviewed all the cases at once."

Terry threw up his arms and took a few steps away. "So, what does all this mean?"

Jennifer walked over to Terry and put her hands on his shoulders. "It tells us that the killer knew how police agencies operated and knew the geography of the southwestern part of this state. It means we are looking for someone who probably worked in law enforcement or with them."

"If he's a cop, then Becky is in greater danger than we thought."

Jennifer rubbed her hands up and down Terry's arms. "So are you. So are you."

CHAPTER FORTY-THREE
[day fourteen]

Paula gave the sofa a gentle kick, waking up Cindy. "Hope you slept well," Paula added as she handed Cindy a cup of coffee. "Hope you take it black. If you want cream and sugar, you're going to be disappointed."

Cindy groaned as she sat up. "Black is fine."

"How are you feeling? I know it was uncomfortable sleeping on the couch."

"No, it's fine. I sleep okay. Truthfully, I feel a lot better, safer."

Paula nodded. "Well, I may ruin that for you."

Cindy sat up a little straighter and lowered her coffee to her lap. "What do you mean?"

Paula sat down next to Cindy. "If you're up to it, I have a way to capture this monster that attacked you and killed the others. But I must stress, there is a risk. However, I will be with you every step of the way."

Cindy looked into her coffee. "You want me to be bait. You're hoping to bring him out and catch him when he tries to kill me."

Paula nodded. "It won't be just me. I'm sure Detective Marshall and Freedman will help us. Between the three of us, you'll be safe. But if you don't want to do this, then it's okay."

"If I don't, then I have to live in fear for the rest of my life," Cindy said with a small sob. "Also, I want my family back home. I don't know if I can do it, but I would like to try. I want this man in prison. I don't want my past to come back to haunt me or hurt my family."

"Let's start with breakfast. Then, we'll pick up your car and bring it back here. After that, we'll go to the police station and talk to Marshall and Freedman."

∞∞∞∞∞∞

Marshall repeatedly tapped his pen on a pad of paper on his desk. Freedman leaned back in his chair and interlocked his hands behind his head. Paula and Cindy sat in front of the detectives.

"What do you think?" Paula asked.

"I don't see how it's going to work," Marshall answered. "How are you going to get Belanger to take the bait? He's had years to come after Ms. Doss and he hasn't. Why would he come after her now?"

Cindy cleared her throat. "I think he's already coming after me. A couple of days ago, someone broke into my house. I think he was searching for something. I found things moved, but nothing was taken."

"And we'll make sure he knows Cindy can identify him," Paula replied. "I'm going to get the *City Times* to publish a story about a witness coming forward. They'll include the part about her being attacked and rescued by a stranger at a hotel. Then, I'll make sure he sees her. We'll drive by his house, go to where he goes shopping, etc. Meanwhile, you and those detectives upstairs will be following us. When he makes his move, you rush in and take him into custody."

"It might work," Freedman interjected. "At least it will keep him from looking for that reporter who was shot a couple of weeks ago."

"Her name is Becky," Paula stated. "But this only works if we can get you guys to cover our backs."

Marshall put his pen down. "Are you sure you can get the paper to print the story? I've never gotten warm fuzzies from them."

"I have an in," Paula replied. "Besides, with Becky being shot and Terry being attacked, I'm sure the paper will cooperate. Also, the story is true, so there shouldn't be a problem."

Marshall looked at Freedman, then back to Paula. "Okay, let's go with your idea. I'll see if I can't get Detectives Gunn and Oha to join us."

Paula stood up and motioned for Cindy to join her. "And I'll get the paper to print the story."

∞ ∞ ∞ ∞ ∞

Terry was smiling as he typed up the story.

The power of the press has won. Because of the previous stories about the vicious attacks on our reporters, a witness has come forward. This woman was also a victim of the assailant, although many years ago. Fortunately, a man staying at the same hotel intervened, saving the woman's life. The police now have a witness who can identify the perpetrator of these heinous crimes.

This is what happens when citizens realize working together, they can stop crime and put criminals away. Working together with each other and the police is the first step. And with each step, we strike fear in the criminals who prey on innocent victims. We become a force ensuring offenders face justice. It is the certainty of punishment that deters crime. Let us become that deterrent. Let us join this brave woman and stand up to crime.

CHAPTER FORTY-FOUR
[day fifteen]

Belanger threw the newspaper across the room. *What possible witness could they have? Some hooker I beat up years ago? The statute of limitations expired years ago.* Belanger crossed the living room and looked out his window. He didn't see any cars or police outside. *It's that damn reporter. I've got to find her. I've got to kill her before this goes any further.*

Belanger booted up his computer. He sat down and drummed his fingers on the table while waiting for the program to open up. He searched for the table with the coordinates of each stop the tall blond's car had made. *That witness, her address has to be one of these points. It's probably that house I searched a couple of days ago. But she didn't have any evidence. Or could she?*

He stood up and started pacing. He reminded himself he needed to take deep breaths to calm down. It wouldn't do any good to raise his blood pressure. The breathing didn't help. His pacing increased. He stopped and returned to the chair and stared at the computer.

There were several coordinates on the tracker program. Belanger wrote them down. He then opened up another computer program and started inputting the coordinates. The map showed the location of each one. Belanger eliminated most of them: the police station, the hospital, stores, etc. But two of them were addresses of homes. One of the addresses was the one he stopped at last night. He noticed the tracker was moving. He now had a new target.

∞∞∞∞∞∞

Diana brought donuts and coffee, making her the popular one in the parking lot of Palmer Park on Lincoln Avenue. Surrounding her were Paula, Cindy, Marshall, Freedman, Terry, Jennifer, Oha, Wanda, and Becky.

Marshall grabbed some coffee and signaled for everyone to gather around. "Here's what's going to happen. Ms. Stanford and Ms. Doss are hoping to attract the attention of our suspect by driving around the neighborhood where he lives and shop. Detective Freedman and I will keep track of them. Detective Gunn and Oha will be in a second car. We'll trade off once we spot our suspect. The rest of you should go home. Let us handle this."

Jennifer raised her hand, which still had a donut in it. "I think both of us following Ms. Stanford and Ms. Doss is a waste of gas. I think it would be better if we take up a position in a certain area. If our suspect shows up, then we can take over tailing him. That way, no one car is behind anyone for any length of time."

"That's a good idea," Marshall replied.

"What about us?" Terry interjected. "How can we help?"

"You can't," Marshall insisted. "You're private citizens. I don't want to place you in danger."

"But you're placing Paula and Cindy in danger," Diana pointed out. "We're aware of the situation and are willing to take the risk."

"No," Marshall stated.

"But we want to help," Wanda objected.

Marshall shook his head. "You can help by going home. It's too dangerous to have civilians involved."

"But Paula and Cindy are civilians," Wanda objected again.

"Yes, they are," Marshall conceded. "But we have four detectives covering them. If there are more civilians, it means I need more cops to provide protection and this operation becomes too big and cumbersome. So go home."

Freedman turned to Jennifer and Oha. "Be on the lookout for a black Cadillac SUV, license A-T-I-4-1-9. If you see the vehicle, call us. Also, look out for a gray pickup. That's Belanger's vehicle. Its license number is A-O-L-7-2-9. No one approaches Belanger alone.

Remember, he's killed before, and I'm sure he'll do again if given the chance."

Paula grabbed a donut and a cup of coffee. "Then let's get this show on the road. We have a killer to catch."

∞∞∞∞∞∞

Paula's and Cindy's first route took them past Belanger's house. Paula drove around the neighborhood, passing his house twice within fifteen minutes.

Cindy fidgeted in her seat. "I didn't see a car in his driveway. What do we do now?"

"We think like a person running errands," Paula answered. "If he is, then he'll probably go to places nearby. So, we'll drive through the parking lots of stores and places in this section of town. At the same time, we'll look for his car. Call Marshall and Freedman and let them know what we're doing."

Cindy pulled out her cell phone and informed the detectives of their plan.

∞∞∞∞∞∞

The tracker showed the tall blond's car at Palmer Park. Belanger parked his pickup in the driveway of an empty house. He walked over to the park and hid behind a baseball dugout so that he could watch the group through a pair of binoculars. He smiled. *So, that's their witness. Yeah, I beat her. If some stranger hadn't knocked on the door, I probably would have killed her. But that was years ago. What can she tell them now? Besides, I checked her house. There wasn't anything there tying me to any of the killings. Who cares? She's not a problem. I finally found that damn reporter, the one who caused all this trouble in the first place.*

Belanger watched as the reporter and a heavy-set woman got into a car. He remembered seeing her once at the hospital when he tried to kill the reporter. The woman he attacked years ago got into the car with the tall blond. He watched them pull out of the parking lot. He knew the tracker would tell him where they were. There was no need to follow them.

He waited to follow the car with the reporter. Belanger made it a point to have at least one car between him and his quarry. He soon realized they were heading to one of the locations he noted on his computer. He chuckled. This was going to be easier than he thought.

∞∞∞∞∞

Terry leaned against Diana's car. He kicked a couple rocks, stood up and walked around the parking lot. He kicked some more rocks before grabbing a small brick and throwing it as far as he could into the grassy area next to the lot.

"Sorry to keep you waiting," Diana said with some surprise. "But I wanted to talk to Wanda and Becky before they left. I talked to them for only a few minutes. There's no reason to get upset."

"It's not that," Terry replied. "It's that Paula and Cindy are out there, and the police are hunting for the killer, and we're supposed to go home and do nothing. Becky was shot. I was beaten up. Even Becky's boyfriend got attacked. I'm not going home and do nothing."

"Well, Wanda and Becky are going back to Wanda's place. Do you want to follow them?"

"No, I want to help catch the killer."

Diana crossed her arms and smirked. "Well, looky here. Somebody's feeling his Wheaties this morning."

"Why? Because I'm a dwarf, you don't think I can do anything."

"Hah," Diana shouted. "You saved my life last year when you went up against that serial killer. You've stood up to Ashford, who is always bullying you. It's not your height that is stopping you. It's frustration. You want to do something, but you don't know what."

Terry looked at the ground and took a couple of deep breaths. "You're right. I just want to do something. I don't want this guy to get away with murder and what he's done to Becky and me."

Diana pulled out her car keys. "So, you want to go around and look for this guy?"

"No," Terry said with a look of confidence. "I have a better idea. Let's see if we can't find his car."

"How are we going to do that?"

"I remember Jennifer telling me the killer used two cars," Terry said while holding up two fingers. "One of the cars is his and the other is the one he used when he shot Becky. She said the killer had to park that cars some place where he could switch it out with his own vehicle. If we can find that car, then we can catch the killer when he comes to change cars."

Diana chuckled. "Great idea except we don't know what kind of car to look for."

"Yes, we do. Freedman told us it was a black, Cadillac SUV."

There are lots of black SUVs. How are we going to know which car is the one the killer uses?"

Terry held up his hand. "I wrote down the license plate number."

CHAPTER FORTY-FIVE

Belanger watched as the car with the overweight woman and the blond reporter left the park. He made it back to his truck in time to see their car turn right on the street in front of him. He made it a point to stay a couple of cars behind them. His venture was rewarded. The first stop they made was at the post office. After a few minutes, he smiled. The blond reporter and the other woman returned to their car.

∞∞∞∞∞∞

Paula pulled into the parking lot of a small strip mall. She parked in front of a barber shop and turned off the engine. She motioned for Cindy to get out of the car. Paula joined her. They moved to the back of the car and leaned against the trunk. Her cell phone rang. Paula picked it up and pressed the accept call button. "Yeah, what's up?"

Marshall was on the other end. "Good question. Why did you stop?"

"Figured it might help if we hang out for a bit, make it easier for him to find us. If we keep driving around, we might pass each other without knowing it. If we don't see him after about fifteen or twenty minutes, we can start driving around again."

"Okay," Marshall acknowledged. "In the meantime, we'll drive around. Maybe we'll get lucky."

Paula ended the call. "I hate to say this," Cindy said looking at Paula, "but I have a bad feeling about this. I feel it in my bones, something bad is going to happen."

∞∞∞∞∞∞

Belanger proceeded to the location of the coordinates he recorded from his computer. It was a modest home with open front yards and fenced-in backyards. He parked his pickup truck in the driveway of a house with a for-sale sign in the front yard. He could tell the house was empty. It was still early in the morning, with people leaving their homes to go to work or to school. He would need to wait until traffic slowed down.

∞∞∞∞∞∞

"So, we drive around looking at all the parking lots," Diana said with frustration. "What about the airport? We have to get pay to get in."

"No," Terry answered. "When I talked to Jennifer, she said the killer would want a parking lot where there would be no record of him going in or out of the lot. Also, any parking lots such as college or school, which are monitored by police or security, would be out. He would want a place where he could park, leave the car for several days, and no one would notice."

Diana pursed her lips. "So, we're looking for someplace like Walmart or a supermarket, where lots of people park all the time."

"I don't think so," Terry replied. "If the store employees don't notice it, some car thieves would. No, he would want someplace where there is foot traffic twenty-four hours a day." Terry snapped his fingers and faced Diana. "Of course." Terry grinned. "I know where to look."

∞∞∞∞∞∞

"We've been here long enough," Paula said to Cindy as they got back in and Paula started her car and put it in reverse. She pulled out of her parking space slowly. She was almost out of the parking space when she noticed a car heading towards her. The driver was on her cellphone, not paying attention to where she was going, heading straight for Paula.

Combat taught Paula to react. She knew she had to get out of the way. She floored the gas and shot backwards across the lot, jumping the concrete tire stop. The rear end was over the concrete, but the car was undamaged.

The woman in the other car screeched to a stop. She jumped out of her car. "Are you all right?" she asked.

Paula and Cindy exited the car. "Yeah, we're okay. But we would have been better if you had watched where you were going."

The woman stood a little taller. "There's no need to be rude. No one got hurt and there's no damage."

Paula pointed at her car. "My car is stuck on this concrete hump because you were on your cell instead of focusing on driving."

The woman huffed and returned to her car. "Good luck with your car," she said sarcastically. She got in her car and left.

Paula closed her eyes and took several deep breaths.

Cindy stared at Paula. "What are you doing?"

Paula opened her eyes. "It's something I need to do to keep me from grabbing my pistol and shooting that stupid bitch."

"I didn't realize you had such anger issues."

Paula smiled. "I was being facetious. But I do have a problem with stupid people. The deep breathing helps me calm down." Paula gestured toward the car. "Let's get back on the road. Watch me while I back up a couple of feet. Hopefully, it will give me enough speed to get over that concrete hump."

Paula got in the car. Cindy moved to the rear of the car, remaining where Paula could see her in the driver's mirror. Cindy motioned for Paula to back up. The car slowly moved back two feet until Cindy heard metal scrapping the concrete. She signaled Paula to stop. Paula put the car in drive and stepped on the brake. She revved the engine, took her foot off the brake, and shot forward, driving over the concrete hump.

"Hey, it worked," Cindy shouted.

Paula put the car in park and stepped out. "Let me check things out. Need to make sure nothing's broken."

She walked to the rear of the car, got down on one knee and looked at the undercarriage of the vehicle. On the ground was a small object covered in tape. Paula picked it up. She began to pull the tape off, revealing a magnet and a small circular device.

"I know what that is," Cindy exclaimed. "It's a tracker, like they use for luggage. Someone is tracking us. He knows where we are."

∞∞∞∞∞∞

"Why did you want to come here?" Diana asked. "Who do we need to talk to at the hospital?"

Terry pointed to the cars in the parking lot. "We are looking for a place where the killer can leave a car without it being noticed, and yet not worry about someone breaking into it. This is the perfect place. It's open twenty-four hours a day. You don't need a ticket or anything to record your coming and going. You can easily leave one car and switch to another and no one would notice."

Terry remained silent as Diana drove the car around the parking lot. It didn't take long before they found what they were looking for.

∞∞∞∞∞∞

Marshall pulled into the parking lot of the strip mall to find Paula and Cindy leaning against Paula's car. He and Freedman got out of their car. "What's this about a tracker?" Marshall asked.

Paula held up the device. "Found out this was attached to my car. Don't know how long it's been there. But you can be sure that your suspect knows everything we are doing."

"He's going to find me and my family," Cindy shouted with tears in her voice. "What are we going to do? You need to protect my family. He can't hurt them. They have nothing to do with this."

Marshall put up his hands. "I understand you're scared and you are worried about your family. And yes, we will make sure they are safe. I know it's hard to stay calm, but I assure you, we will keep you and your family safe."

"How?" Cindy asked with fear in her voice.

Freedman took the tracking device from Paula and examined it. "I'll let Detectives Gunn and Oha know about this."

∞∞∞∞∞∞

Jennifer picked up her cell phone. "What's up," She asked.

Marshall was at the other end. "We just found a tracker on Ms. Stanford's car. Freedman and I are with Ms. Stanford and Ms. Doss. So, we have them covered. We need you to make sure the reporter, Ms. Watson is okay."

"Of course," Jennifer replied. "Where is she?"

Marshall hesitated. "According to Ms. Stanford, Ms. Watson went home with her friend. We're going to Ms. Doss's house to check things out. I'll let you know if anything else turns up."

Jennifer ended the call. Her next call was to Terry.

He answered on the second ring. "Jennifer. I was just getting ready to call you."

"I'm flattered," Jennifer replied. "If you're calling to ask me out, your timing sucks."

Terry blushed. "Heh, I wanted to let you know that Diana and I found the black Cadillac SUV you were looking for. It's here in the hospital parking lot. It's in section D."

"Thanks. That's really helpful. But I need to know where your friend, Becky, is. Where is she staying?"

"Why? Isn't the killer chasing Paula and Cindy?"

"They found a tracking device on Ms. Stanford's car. It's possible the killer used it to find out where Ms. Watson is."

"She's at Wanda's house," Terry answered. "It's 618 Redwood Avenue. You can recognize it by the turtle decorations in the front yard."

Jennifer thanked Terry before she ended the call. Terry turned to Diana. "We've got to get to Wanda's. Becky could be in danger, and we have to save her."

"No," Diana shouted. "Call the police. It's their job to protect her."

"They already know." Terry replied. "But we are only ten minutes away. We can help till they get there. Please. Let's go and make sure Becky's safe."

Diana groaned as she put her car in gear and left the hospital parking lot.

∞∞∞∞∞

Belanger yawned. He hadn't realized he had fallen asleep. A look at his watch informed him it was midmorning. He took a few minutes to ensure no one was outside in the neighborhood. He pulled his pistol out of a backpack and placed it in his back pocket. He got out of his pickup and walked along the street, taking note which homes had their doors open or window shades up. He listened for barking dogs. After walking around for ten minutes, he felt safe enough to approach the home where his prey was.

Belanger stopped at the front door. He took a moment to listen for sounds inside of the house. He tried the door and discovered it was locked. He took a deep breath and knocked on the door.

He heard footsteps coming to the door. "Who is it?" said a voice from inside the house.

Belanger pulled a badge from his pocket. "I'm with the police department. I was sent over to make sure you and the reporter were okay."

Becky opened the door. "Wonderful. You're here to protect us."

"Absolutely," Belanger responded. "Mind if I come in?"

Becky opened the door wider and motioned for him to come in. Keiko and Tarzan ran up to Belanger, who stepped back from the dogs. "Excuse me," Belanger begged, holding his hands in front of him to repel the dogs. "Could you do something about the dogs. I'm not really fond of dogs."

"Of course," Becky replied as she grabbed Tarzan by the collar and led him outside into the backyard. She motioned for Keiko to follow. Keiko hesitated until Becky pushed the dog out of the door. Becky closed it but the dogs remained sitting just outside of the door.

"Where's the owner of the house?" Belanger asked.

Becky turned to answer him, but she stopped. "How did you know this isn't my house?"

"Where is she?" Belanger demanded.

"Right here," Wanda shouted. "Now, who are you to come into my house and make demands?"

Belanger pulled out his pistol. "It doesn't matter who I am. What matters is who you are."

"I know who you are," Wanda stated. "You're the man who killed all those women and the one who shot Becky."

"And I remember you," Belanger replied. "I ran into you at the hospital. If you hadn't been there that day, I wouldn't have to do this now." Belanger raised his pistol and motioned for the two women to move next to the sofa.

"Are you here to kill us?" Becky asked with defiance. "You do know that the police know who you are. They are collecting evidence that you committed all those murders years ago right now. Killing us will only make things worse."

"Yeah, yeah," Belanger scoffed. "What evidence. That package some hooker sent you. I've destroyed that. Unless you dug up something. What did you find out?"

Someone knocking on the front door stopped Becky from answering. With the pistol, Belanger motioned for Wanda to answer the door. "Don't do anything stupid," he said. "I have enough bullets in this thing for everyone."

Wanda went to the door. She opened the door a few inches.

"We're here to help you," Terry exclaimed as he muscled his way into Wanda's house. Diana followed Terry in. They moved past Wanda, only to stop when they saw Belanger pointing a pistol at them.

"You should have stayed out," Belanger said, waving his pistol at Terry and Diana. "Poking your nose into this makes things complicated." Belanger motioned for Terry, Diana, and Wanda to join Becky in the living room. He forced them to move toward the door leading to the backyard.

The four of them faced Belanger. "What are you going to do?" Terry asked. "You can't kill all of us. The police already know who you are. And four more bodies will not help you. In fact, it will make things worse for you."

"Well, I really don't have a choice," Belanger responded. "You all couldn't leave things alone. You had to poke your nose into things that happened years ago. It was the past. It didn't matter anymore."

"Yes, it did," Wanda yelled as she grabbed a stuffed turtle and held it up in front of her. Wanda stepped in front of Becky. "You can't shoot us. You'll never get away with killing us. You'll only end up in prison for the rest of your life."

"She's right," Terry said as he surreptitiously took a step toward the sliding door leading to the backyard where Keiko and Tarzan were barking. "The police are on their way here right now. I'll bet they'll be knocking on door any second."

Belanger turned his head and glanced at the door.

That slight distraction was all Terry needed to grab the sliding door and let the dogs in. Belanger turned his attention to the dogs, pointing his pistol at them. Keiko charged while Tarzan sought shelter behind her mistress. Wanda took a step forward and threw the stuffed turtle at him, deflecting his aim. He quickly regained his position, but it was too late.

No one knew if Keiko was a full-blooded German shepherd or not, but she had the speed, strength, and powerful jaws of one. She jumped up and clamped down on Belanger's arm, forcing it down. He fired the gun a second time. The bullet hit the floor. Keiko began pulling Belanger away from Terry and the others. Blood flowed from the wound Keiko was inflicting. She was not letting go, no matter how much Belanger screamed from the pain. Keiko's attack gave Tarzan courage and he joined the assault, biting and pulling on Belanger's pants' leg.

Terry grabbed Diana and the others, herding them out of the house. They ran through the backyard, around the house and into the front where they met Jennifer and Oha. "Quick," Terry shouted. "The killer is in the house." Terry turned to lead the two detectives into the house through the back door.

Jennifer pushed Terry aside as she and Oha entered the home. Keiko still had hold of Belanger's arm. Tarzan was barking at him. "Get this dog off of me," Belanger cried. "It's going to take my arm off."

Oha had his weapon out. "How do we get the dog off of him? Should I shoot the dog?" he said, looking to Jennifer for guidance.

"No," Terry commanded. "I'll get Keiko to let him go. But first, he needs to drop his gun."

Belanger growled at Terry, but he dropped his pistol. Terry went over to it, picked it up, and handed it to Jennifer. He grabbed Keiko's collar and pulled her. Tarzan backed away. Keiko let go in an effort to get a better bite, but Terry pulled her away before she could. He stared at Belanger. "Do as the detectives say, or I'll release Keiko again. And this time, no one is going to get her to let go."

"You think you're so smart," Belanger bellowed. "What have you got? Me threatening you with a weapon? I'll make a plea deal and be out in six months."

Jennifer snickered. "I love his confidence." She held up his pistol. "I'm willing to bet this is the same weapon that killed Tawana Williams and was used to shoot Ms. Watson. And there are the homicides you committed all those years ago."

"How are you going to prove I committed any homicides? With fingerprints? Ballistics? There's no way."

"Actually," Jennifer continued, "I intend to do it with DNA. And no, I don't need a warrant. There's enough of your blood at this crime scene for us to get a very good sample."

Belanger stared at the detective and glared at Terry. "If it hadn't been for you and that reporter, none of this would have happened."

Terry stepped in front of Belanger. "Wrong. If it hadn't been for Becky, you would have gotten away with murder."

EPILOGUE

"It's great things are back to normal." Becky said as she took a sip from her drink of ginger ale before setting it down on the table she shared with Terry and Paula in Murphy's. "I got a call from Cindy Doss. Her family is back and the kids are back in school. She also told them about her life before she met her husband and why they had to visit their grandparents. Then she told them about how she helped the police catch the killer. Her kids think she's a hero."

"She is," Paula replied. "It takes courage to act when you're scared. But she did great."

"I'm just glad I can come here to Murphy's without worrying about getting mugged," Terry replied. He looked over at Paula. "What's wrong? Why aren't you drinking?"

Paula glanced at Terry before staring at the drink in front of her. "It's that damn VA counselor. She's got me thinking that I'm becoming an alcoholic. So, I'm drinking ginger ale."

"Are you really an alcoholic?" Becky asked. "I've never seen you out of control when you're not drinking."

"I honestly don't know. I know I like drinking. It helps me calm down. But do I need it? Can I go without it? I really don't know what to do."

Terry took a sip of his beer. "You're going to hate me, but I suggest you talk this over with your counselor. She's probably the only one who can help you."

"Great, you're all here," bellowed Fitch as he approached the table. "Did Terry tell you the good news?"

"You won the lottery," Paula answered sarcastically as she picked up her drink. She looked at it and put it down.

Fitch pulled out a chair and sat down. "Well, you've a lot to celebrate. Turns out you get the ten-thousand-dollar reward the paper offered for anyone who helped catch the person who shot Becky."

Paula leaned back in her chair. "Not that I don't like money, but I had nothing to do with capturing Belanger."

"True," Fitch acknowledged. "There were five involved with his capture. Four of them are employees of the newspaper, so they aren't eligible for the reward. The one who really did capture Belanger and save the others was your dog."

"Keiko," a surprised Paula responded. "You're giving ten thousand dollars to a dog. Give her a bunch of dog biscuits and save yourself some money."

Fitch laughed. "The money goes to you. After all, she's your dog. Besides, with the reward money, it might help you get a loan so that you can buy the gym."

Paula shook her head. "Thanks. But even with that money, I won't have enough. The gym is valued at seven hundred and fifty thousand dollars. I need at least ten percent of that before I can get a loan."

"How about a partner?" Terry asked as he lifted his beer

"The partner will have to come up with at least thirty-five thousand dollars. Who has that kind of money to invest in a gym which may or may not make it?"

"I do," Terry answered as he lowered his beer and leaned forward. "I know you and I know you will do everything you can to make that gym successful. I even went over the books with the owner and it's a sound investment."

Paula let out a deep breath. Again, she stared at her drink. "Why would you do that? What do you know about running a gym?"

Terry shook his head. "Nothing. But I know a little about business management. And I have a lot of faith in you. Think about it I'll meet you at the bank tomorrow morning at ten to set up the loan. We can talk about it with them and see if there are any issues. As for me, I'm sure we can manage it. After all, look how well we've been doing so far."

"So far, we've managed to get one person shot, you beat up, and a group of you held at gunpoint. Not exactly batting a thousand."

"And we solved a bunch of cold cases and caught a murderer Now, if you will excuse me, I have a previous appointment." Terry gave everyone a mock salute as he left.

∞∞∞∞∞

Jennifer waved as Terry walked into the Pink Lily Lounge. Terry nodded as he made his way to the table where Jennifer was waiting.

Jennifer toyed with her drink. "Nice place. Why did you want to meet here?"

"Needed to find out if you were a jazz fan," Terry replied.

Jennifer shrugged her shoulders. "It's okay. I'm more into old-time rock-and-roll. You know, the music from the 50s and 60s. But I also like some of the music from the 70s and 80s. What about you?"

"Big band era. Kristen loved it. Sorry, I didn't mean to bring her up."

Jennifer reached over and grasped Terry's hand. "She was your wife. I think it's nice that you still care for her. Still, I'm hoping I can get you to care for me too."

Terry returned her grasp. "I'm beginning to."

"So, you brought me here to see if I like jazz."

"Not really," Terry replied. "One of the women Becky interviewed worked here before Belanger killed her. I thought the least I should do is see where she worked. Kind of honoring her in some small way."

Jennifer leaned over and kissed Terry. "I think you are really sweet."

Terry chuckled. "This is coming from a detective who deals with murderers every day. That reminds me. What about Belanger?"

Jennifer smiled as she took a sip from her drink. "Once he was confronted with the evidence we had against him, he confessed. We had the weapon he used to killed Tawana Williams and shoot your friend. There was DNA evidence from several of the cold cases. There was the video we had of him attacking you and then a juvenile also came forward and stated he saw the attack added to the evidence we had against him. He knew we had him. He also confessed to burglarizing your friend's and Ms. Doss's homes. I'm sure he'll make some kind of deal with the DA; but I'm also sure he'll spend the rest of his life in prison."

"What I can't figure out is why he stopped killing all those years ago. I know why he started again. It was because Tawana Williams sent that package to Becky. But why did he stop?"

"He had prostate cancer," Jennifer answered. "He had his prostate removed and I guess it killed his sex drive. At least that's what he said."

"At least we don't have to worry about him anymore."

Jennifer stared at Terry. "Let's not worry about killers, crime, murder, or mayhem. Let's focus on having a good night."

Terry reached over and gave Jennifer a kiss.

THE END

ACKNOWLEDGMENTS

In April of 2018, I came across an article on the internet about a Jane Doe identified 37 years after she was murdered. The woman was identified through the DNA Doe Project, an organization dedicated to helping law enforcement agencies and medical examiners identify their John and Jane Does so the families of these victims can be reunited with their loved ones.

What caught my eye was one of the first departments to benefit from the project was the Miami County Sheriff's Office in Ohio. Fortunately, my good friend and Marine Buddy, David Norman worked there. Captain Norman provided me with the facts of the case that had been released to the public. Because it was still an open case, there were some things he was not permitted to reveal. Being a former military police officer, I am aware of the need to NOT discuss active investigations with those outside of the investigation. Still, I want to recognize Captain Norman and the Miami County Sheriff's Office, as well as other law enforcement agencies, for taking proactive measures to resolve cold cases. Their dedication to these cases is a credit to law enforcement,

I also want to thank the DNA Doe Project, which now has provided identification for so many John and Jane Does and continues to do so. Special thanks go out to Sue Grafton, whose book Q is for Quarry, inspired Margaret Press, and later Colleen Fitzpatrick, to set up the DNA Doe Project to use genetic genealogy to help identify so many unknown victims in our society. Currently, they are working on about

250 cases. Their task is never done. You can find out more about this organization at https://dnadoeproject.org .

Then there is KaylaMae Smith, who helped proofread the manuscript. Her insights proved valuable. She also used her talent to design the cover for this novel.

I also need to thank my friend and wife, Hiromi, for her support and assistance with proofreading this novel and my writing endeavors.

For all those fellow writers who encouraged me and for my many readers, thank you for your support.

About the Author

Mark Zeid spent seven years on active duty as a military police officer for the U.S. Marine Corps. After the Marines, he went to college and grad school, which led him to working and living in Japan for 25 years. During which time he taught English for Japanese schools and criminal justice for a satellite college on military bases. He also published more than 600 articles in various military, educational, and local news publications. Mark Zeid retired from the Marine Corps Reserves in 2004. Upon returning to the United States, he worked at the Center for Domestic Preparedness, a training facility run by Homeland Security for first responders. He was deployed several times to help with disaster recovery efforts in the United States. Currently retired, Mark Zeid teaches writing classes and Holocaust education.

His novels are inspired by actual criminal events. He has had four mystery novels published, two of which won local awards. He publishes the first chapter of his novels on his website at

https://zeidsmysteries.com

Thank you for reading.
Please review this book. Reviews help others find
Absolutely Amazing eBooks and inspire us to keep
providing these marvelous tales.
If you would like to be put on our email list to receive
updates on new releases, contests, and promotions, please
go to AbsolutelyAmazingEbooks.com and sign up.

AbsolutelyAmazingEbooks.com

or AA-eBooks.com

For sales, editorial information, subsidiary rights information
or a catalog, please write or phone or e-mail
AbsolutelyAmazingEbooks
Manhanset House
Shelter Island Hts., New York 11965-0342, US
Tel: 212-427-7139
www.AbsolutelyAmazingEbooks.com
bricktower@aol.com
www.IngramContent.com